COLD HANDS, WARM HEARTS

Other Available Books by Jenny Jacobs:

Love by Design

COLD HANDS, WARM HEARTS

•

Jenny Jacobs

AVALON BOOKS
NEW YORK

© Copyright 2010 by Jennifer Lawler
All rights reserved.
All the characters in the book are fictitious,
and any resemblance to actual persons,
living or dead, is purely coincidental.
Published by Thomas Bouregy & Co., Inc.
160 Madison Avenue, New York, NY 10016

Library of Congress Cataloging-in-Publication Data

Jacobs, Jenny, 1965–
  Cold hands, warm hearts / Jenny Jacobs.
      p. cm.
  ISBN 978-0-8034-7775-9 (acid-free paper)   1. Single mothers—Fiction.   2. Mothers and daughters—Fiction.   3. United States, Federal Bureau of Investigation—Employees—Fiction.   4. Minnesota—Fiction.   I. Title.
  PS3612.A94435C65 2010
  813'.6—dc22
                                                    2010006230

PRINTED IN THE UNITED STATES OF AMERICA
ON ACID-FREE PAPER
BY HADDON CRAFTSMEN, BLOOMSBURG, PENNSYLVANIA

For Jessica, the very best writer in the world.
And a pretty wonderful daughter too.

Chapter One

It was this or live in her car, Char reminded herself as she stared at the weather through the windshield of her little Ford. She'd repeated that thought like a mantra all the way from the Twin Cities, following Keith's monster pickup truck north on I-35, her own small economy car bucking on the ice and snow. The handyman's heavy truck, equipped with four-wheel drive, zoomed unconcernedly through the traffic as they wound their way through the thicket of interchanges that saw them past St. Paul, then headed ever farther north, veering from interstate highways to state highways to county roads, the level of road maintenance deteriorating as they traveled farther and farther away from civilization. Her fingers clutched the steering wheel until her knuckles turned white and her palms ached from the effort.

The ribbon of road twisted, icy and slick, through thick stands of birch and pine that towered overhead and stretched as far as the eye could see, blocking the sun and casting the road into a perpetual gloom that made it even more difficult to navigate.

Cinnamon trembled in the seat next to her and whined

in anxiety. Char gritted her teeth against the sound. She didn't dare lift a finger from the steering wheel to run a soothing hand down the little Pomeranian's back. She settled for a halfhearted, "Easy, girl, it's going to be okay." The words didn't make either of them feel better, so she lapsed into silence, squinting out the windshield, trying to see through the spitting snow as they bounced over the rutted asphalt.

Several hours after they'd left the hospital, they were nearing the end of the trip. Keith finally turned off onto a gravel road. Thankful, she followed him down a steep incline, the rough surface jarring her teeth as she fought her way down it. She clenched her jaw tighter as she made a sharp and unexpected turn and her little red car skidded toward a ditch. Char closed her eyes and didn't fight the skid, just hoped the crash wouldn't injure her too badly. The car righted itself in time, and she coasted to a stop in the driveway next to Keith's truck.

Unsticking one finger at a time from the steering wheel, she leaned back in the seat for a moment. The adventure wasn't over yet—it had just started. Wearily, she pushed the car door open and stepped out into ankle-deep snow. She sighed as it melted over the tops of her tennis shoes. Keith had already warned her that she was singularly ill-equipped for this "camping trip," as he'd insisted on referring to it. He didn't seem to understand how desperately she needed a place to stay.

When she'd called the real estate agent on the phone, and he'd told her that, as far as he knew, the tiny cabin that she'd inherited from her aunt was still habitable, she'd thought she might break down and weep. Aunt Kay had worked as a secretary for a Minneapolis corporation for many years, and at her death she'd left a tiny estate that consisted mostly of the old summer cabin and a few thousand dollars in savings. Everything had gone to Char.

Aunt Kay had died almost two years before, and Char had tucked the money and the deed away, never realizing that one day it would come to this. It was almost as if her beloved Aunt Kay, the last member of her family, had known she'd need one final bit of help to see her through.

Now, looking at the cabin, the setting sun revealing peeling paint and warped siding, the screen door banging forlornly in the wind, she wondered if living in her car might not have been the better idea. Keith, who was the real estate agent's brother as well as the caretaker he'd recommended for Char to hire, swung down from his pickup and gave her a big grin, awaiting her reaction.

More towering pines and birch trees surrounded the cabin. A clearing in front of the building allowed a view of the lakeshore, not more than one hundred yards away. Wind creaked through the trees, and waves lapped the shoreline. Cold and snow and ice, gray skies, gray lake, gray cabin.

"I like how you tried to lose me in St. Paul," Char said, plastering a smile onto her face. Bravado, that was the key. If she let the full reality of the situation sink in—how precarious it was, how very close to disaster she balanced—she'd never be able to do it. People with plenty of options never understood how you could get to the last one. When you said you didn't have any money, they thought you meant you were down to your last ten thousand bucks. They had no idea that you meant the twelve dollars in your pocket and a few hundred dollars in the bank. That was it—no credit cards, no home equity lines of credit, nothing. A few hundred dollars and a well-used Ford and more thousands of dollars in medical bills than she could possibly pay back.

Keith's grin broadened. "I wasn't trying to lose you," he said. "Getting lost just seems to come natural to you."

"Oh, ha," she said. There was something about her that made men treat her like a little sister. Possibly it was because she was short, with corkscrews of auburn curls springing from her head, a dusting of freckles over her nose and cheeks. She *looked* like a little sister.

Pocketing her car keys and shutting the car door carefully so as not to wake Cinnamon, who had finally—and not a moment too soon—given up whining and now curled up with her nose tucked into her tail, Char squared her shoulders and took a step toward the cabin.

"Gonna be a lot of work getting it ready for the winter," Keith said.

"I'm not afraid of hard work," she said.

He shook his head, already assuming he was going to do most of the work, and swung the tailgate open. He started undoing the straps holding the tarpaulin down, uncovering the boxes in the back of the pickup, all of her and Abby's worldly possessions.

"Let's get this unloaded," he said. "Then I'll show you around the property, and you can start making a list of what you need."

She hoped she wouldn't need much, because her twelve dollars wasn't going to stretch very far. She lifted a box from the bed of the truck and followed Keith into the cabin, delighted to see a surprisingly comfortable interior. The cabin had one main room, along with a tiny alcove in a corner that had probably once been a storage closet but that had

Cold Hands, Warm Hearts 5

been turned into a tiny bedroom, a small galley kitchen and, to her vast relief, an indoor bathroom. She'd seen the outhouse set back in the trees and feared the worst. She could just imagine trying to explain that to Abby.

Her mind skittered away from her daughter. She couldn't think about that right now. Abby was still in the hospital while Char and Keith were up here making the cabin habitable for the winter. *Everything is going to be all right.* Her other mantra. She just wished she believed it.

Keith dumped the box he carried onto the floor in the main living area. "I don't know," he said, his voice low and worried. "Char, you could get snowed in here, and if your kid needed something—"

Dread hit Char in the pit of her stomach. "I've thought of that," she said, keeping her voice firm and neutral. "I've already talked to a guy in Grand Rapids who plows driveways for a living. He'll make sure we can get out of here if we need to."

"Have you really thought this through?"

"Yes," Char said, hating the sound of the whine in her voice. "It's going to be okay." She smiled to take the edge off.

Keith just shook his head again and walked back outside. Hoping she'd won that round, Char followed him out. "Old lady Wilson's family owns all of that," Keith said, waving a hand to the north. Char was grateful for the change of subject. "When this area gets more developed, they're going to make a fortune selling it off." He shook his head at the luck of some people. "You won't see any of these folks all winter." He gave her a glance. "You sure you're up for this?"

"I'm sure," she said, and she would have felt better if her voice hadn't shaken so much as she said it.

Long after dark, Char pulled into the hospital parking lot and got out of the car, slamming the door shut behind her. The drive from up north had taken longer than she'd thought. Everything always took longer. She'd called the hospital from a gas station in St. Paul and given an ETA, which she'd missed. Abby would be sure to let her know about it.

She pushed open the hospital's revolving door, nodded at the guard on duty, then stepped into the elevator. *Everything is going to be all right,* she told herself. She used to sing a song like that to Abby. *Everything is going to be all right, punkin' pie.* She used to sing it and hope that one of them would believe it. She didn't particularly care which one it was. She wondered if either one of them would believe it now.

On the seventh floor, she pushed the door to her daughter's room open and saw Abby, dressed and sitting up in bed, directing Regina, her favorite nurse, who was packing up Abby's clothes and belongings: toys and books and half-deflated balloons—all detritus of an extended stay in the children's surgical unit of a hospital. Char's shoulders relaxed in relief at the sight of her brown-haired, brown-eyed little girl, her tipped-up nose so like Char's own, her wide smile seen more often these days than Char's. In the first days after surgery, she'd been so still and unmoving, she'd scared Char half to death.

"Dakota stays with me," Abby said, reaching for the stuffed wolf Regina was about to toss into a duffel bag and clamping it under her arm. "And I want to wear the pink sweater."

"Hey, punkin'." Char felt herself breathe for what seemed like the first time all day. "You've already got a sweater on."

"Mama!" Abby yelled, motioning at her frantically. Char saw that the nurse had taken the bandage off Abby's head. The scar was prominent, red and raw looking. The surgeons had shaved most of the hair off one side of her head, and her skull looked pale and fragile. Char still wasn't used to it. When Abby reached for her, Char saw that the IV in her arm had finally been removed. Char dropped her purse onto the bed and hugged Abby, gently at first because the scars were so red and scary and everything was so delicate and tenuous, but Abby's thin, wiry arms pulled her tight, squeezing the breath out of her. She placed a gentle kiss on Abby's forehead and felt the tears welling up again. The worst was over, and still she couldn't stop the tears. She cried so unexpectedly and often these days that she was afraid it might become one of the more annoying of her character flaws.

"How'd it go?" Regina asked, zipping the duffel bag closed, not mentioning the tears, which Char appreciated. Regina was an older, taller, sturdier woman who'd taken a shine to Abby, and Abby had exuberantly returned the favor.

"Oh, fine," Char said. "It's going to be perfect, Regina. We got everything all ready—oil in the heater tank, backup generator in service. I'll be able to get some writing done, and Abby will be able to rest and recover. We're all set."

"Good," Regina said, although she was frowning and had her hands on her hips. "I'm still not sure—"

"We're going to be fine."

"What are you talking about?" Abby wanted to know, letting go of Char and pushing her back so she could look up into her face.

Char took a deep breath. She'd better handle this just right or she'd disrupt Abby's already precarious emotional balance. Her daughter was only eight years old, for heaven's sake. She shouldn't have to deal with this—not any of it. "You remember that Aunt Kay died a few years ago, and she gave us her lake cabin?" Char asked.

"Yeah," Abby said suspiciously, narrowing her eyes. They'd never been to the cabin because it was so far from home. Reclusive Aunt Kay had only occasionally deigned to have company at her Minneapolis apartment, so Abby had never known her very well. No wonder she was suspicious.

"We're going to live there this winter." Char forced a cheery tone into her voice, as if this was a treat, an adventure, not a desperate, last-gasp effort to keep everything together.

"At the cabin?"

"Yes." Then, hurrying to convince her, she added, "It belonged to Aunt Kay's husband, Uncle Ned. He died before you were born. It was his fishing cabin." She let her voice trail off at Abby's expression.

"What happened to the blue house?"

"You know what happened to the blue house."

"Tell me what happened to the blue house," Abby demanded, her voice rising. Char sensed her daughter's fear and panic rising along with her voice. So much for making it sound like a treat. She hurried to reassure Abby, sitting down on the bed and stroking her daughter's arm to soothe her. Abby snatched her arm away, folded both arms across her chest, and glared at Char.

"We sold the blue house when Mommy and Daddy decided to get a divorce," Char said, and she marveled at how steady and neutral her voice sounded. The divorce had happened three years earlier. While Abby didn't remember much about her life before then, she did remember living in the blue house, Char knew. Char and Theodore hadn't built much equity in the house, though, and after the real estate agent's fees, there had been very little profit to share after the sale. Char hadn't wanted the burden of trying to make mortgage payments, so she'd agreed for them to sell it. Later she realized that even then Theodore had been trying to turn all of his assets into cash.

He'd agreed in the divorce settlement to pay Abby's health insurance, which he could get through his job. But when he skipped town . . .

Suddenly the room seemed very cold, and Char shivered. Skipped town or—?

"What happened to the green house?" Abby asked, her voice as steely as an eight-year-old could manage.

"We didn't own the green house," Char said, closing her eyes. The green house was one side of a small rental duplex in not your best part of town where they'd moved after the divorce. When Abby's illness was diagnosed and Char discovered there was no insurance, she'd sublet the place out. Her friend Deanna back home had sold everything in it to help pay the medical bills.

"What happened to the green house?" Abby would not be deterred. She was breathing faster. She was going to start hyperventilating, and then Regina was going to get mad at Char. . . .

"Someone else is living there now," Char said. "You know that. Remember how we said good-bye before we drove all the way up here for your surgery?"

"I thought we were going back," Abby said, even though Char had told her several times, as gently as she could, that that wasn't happening.

"Someone else is living there now," she repeated.

"Why not us?" Abby demanded.

"We can't afford it," Char said flatly. She didn't mention the other reason, the fear that had driven her from their home. When Theodore had disappeared, she no longer felt safe living there. She told herself that he was unreliable, that he had simply run off, run away, and there was nothing shocking about that. Still, the question was, *why*? He'd left behind a thriving legal practice, a *daughter*. She worried that his absence could only be for an unpleasant reason. In itself, that was bad enough, but Theodore had always had a genius for dragging her into his unpleasantness too.

She didn't think he had any way of knowing about her newly inherited cabin. Not only was it hundreds of miles from home, but it was remote. No one would find them there. It seemed a safer place to be than the duplex she and Abby had been living in—at least until he reappeared and explained what had happened. *If* he showed up again. If his disappearance could be explained.

"Why can't we live with Daddy?" Abby asked now.

"I don't know where Daddy is," Char said, the familiar wave of inadequacy and anger washing over her. She'd already explained to Abby that her daddy had a problem that he had to solve and that, once he did, he would be able to be part of Abby's life again. That explanation was the best

Cold Hands, Warm Hearts

Char could do. She had no idea why Theodore had done what he'd done. Any reasons he gave would be self-serving. It used to outrage her, how he blamed his problems on other people, including Char, but now she knew that outrage didn't help. All she could do was try to minimize the damage he inflicted.

"I miss Daddy."

"I know you do, honey."

"I'm not 'honey,' " Abby said crossly. "I'm 'beautiful.' "

"Okay, beautiful," Char said gamely.

"Did you want the purple socks or the pink ones?" Regina finally butted in, coming back from the window, where she'd waited for them to have their conversation. She held up both pairs of socks. Char watched gratefully as Regina jollied the little girl into a better mood without making a big production of her efforts.

They had a place to live and a little time to get back on their feet. *We'd better make it,* Char thought. *We have to make it.*

Char surveyed the pile of logs with satisfaction. They were by no means uniform in length, but they looked like logs, and they'd burn like logs, if it came to that. Keith had warned her that the cabin's furnace was unreliable, especially during the sudden, severe snowstorms common to the area, and she prided herself on preparing for the worst. If only she'd prepared for the worst *before*—

She shoved the thought away as she opened the exterior cellar doors and climbed the six steps down. In the cellar, she found a heavy wooden box, which she carried outside. Loading the box with logs, she hauled it back down, then dumped the load in a corner by the wood-burning furnace that supplemented the oil burner. After a few trips, she decided she'd done enough manual labor for one morning. Time for a break.

"Ready for hot chocolate?" she called to Abby, who was bundled up by the lakeshore, throwing stones into the gently lapping water. Keith had said the lake would freeze over by Thanksgiving, but that didn't seem possible. There was a great deal of water. But then, he'd warned her that there would be a great deal of cold. Abby looked up from her stone-throwing game and trotted over.

"Where's Cinnamon?" Char asked. The little dog could usually be found right at Abby's heels.

"I don't know."

Char glanced around the yard but saw no sign of the Pomeranian. Little Cinnamon was much too small and vulnerable to wander outside unsupervised, especially here. A fox or wolf would think she was lunch. What had Char been thinking? She should never have let Cinnamon out while she was distracted with chores. Keith was right. She wasn't ready for this.

"When did you see her last?" Char asked.

"I don't remember," Abby said, her face crumpling. "I don't know!"

Char could tell Abby was near tears. "We'll find her, honey," she said, with more confidence than she felt. "Come on, let's see if she's in back." She reached down to take Abby's hand.

Abby nodded, and they headed in that direction. "Cinny!" she shouted, as they rounded the corner of the cabin. "Cinny, come here! Good girl! Come here!"

Char heard the faint bark of the dog. She hurried forward, Abby close at her heels. She pushed through a tangle of bushes near the rear of Mrs. Wilson's cabin, which was more of a small lake home than a cabin like the one she'd inherited.

"Stay back, Abby," she warned as a thorn caught the sleeve of her coat. Grateful for her work gloves, she pushed deeper into the mass of dead brush. Her ankle twisted slightly as she slipped on the frozen ground. Hearing a soft whimper close by, she looked down and saw a deeply dug window well into which Cinnamon had fallen. Not only had the plastic cover been removed, but the window it was supposed to protect had been broken—not by Cinnamon, but by some other animal, or maybe a person.

"You silly puppy!" Char crooned, kneeling down to rescue the dog. "What were you chasing?" Cinnamon whimpered again as Char lifted her out. Crouching on the ground, Char ran her hands gently over the dog, who yelped when she touched a hind leg.

"She hurt her leg," Char said to Abby, who hadn't listened to her instructions and was leaning over her shoulder. She got to her feet with the dog in her arms.

"Is she going to be okay?" Abby asked, the anxiety clear in her voice.

"I'm sure she'll be fine," Char said. She'd said the words just like that for so long, they came without thinking, and she didn't even know if they were true or not anymore. From the look on Abby's face, her daughter didn't know either. "We'll bring her to the vet."

"Now?" Abby demanded.

Char looked down at her daughter's white, pinched face. She thought of the twelve dollars in her pocket. "Now," she sighed. How she'd pay for it, she'd worry about later.

* * *

"This is the vet's?" Abby asked. The low wooden building had seen better days. If it had ever boasted paint, it was long gone. The wooden sign extending from a pole was cracked across the face. Even so, Dr. Wilson had come highly recommended. Actually, Keith had said he was competent and close, and that had been good enough for Char, considering the lack of alternatives.

To Abby, Char said, "This is it," and she pushed open the door. The scrupulously clean interior reassured her. She ignored the cracked vinyl flooring and took a seat in one of the molded plastic chairs, settling Cinnamon on her lap. Abby sat next to her. No one else was in the waiting room.

An interior door burst open, and a young redheaded woman came through at top speed, pulling up short when she saw them. "Hi, I'm Kate, Dr. Wilson's assistant. What's up?" She flicked a glance at Abby, who'd pulled off her hat, her raw, red scar a beacon of difference. Kate didn't ask about it, for which Char was grateful. With her emotions still so close to the surface, it was hard to talk about what had happened.

"I'm Char Simmons. This is my daughter, Abby. Our dog was injured," Char said, gauging the fast-talking redhead accurately and deciding details could wait.

"This the dog?" Kate asked, approaching. "A Pom!" she exclaimed. "We don't get too many Poms around here. They don't pull their own weight."

"She's a great dog," Abby said fiercely, jumping to her feet and rounding on Kate.

"Sorry, sorry," Kate said, holding up a hand in surrender. "Most of the companion animals around here are hunting dogs or working dogs." She waved for them to follow her

Cold Hands, Warm Hearts 15

into the back, then opened the door to an exam room and patted the table. "You want to put her here, please?"

Gently, Char placed Cinnamon on the table. Kate ran competent but kind hands across the dog's body, then moved to the hallway. "Dad! Dad! Come in here."

After a moment, a tall, gray-haired man strode into the room, stopping in his tracks at the sight of the dog on the table.

"A Pomeranian? Who owns a Pomeranian?" he demanded. Then he caught sight of Char and Abby. "This yours?" he said.

"Yes," Char said meekly. Apparently she should have brought a retriever or a malamute.

"This is Char Simmons and her daughter, Abby," Kate explained.

"And that's Cinnamon," Abby piped up. "She's a great dog," she added loyally, to cut off any potential insults that might be forthcoming.

"You bet she is," Dr. Wilson said, going to the sink and washing his hands. "Pomeranians are excellent watchdogs."

"Yes," Abby agreed. "She's very brave."

She's too stupid to know she's a tenth the size of the dogs she runs off the property, Char thought but didn't say.

"We just moved up here," was what she did say. "She wandered onto a neighbor's property and fell into a window well and hurt her leg." She realized with a jolt that the neighbor's property she was talking about belonged to Dr. Wilson's family. Keith had mentioned as much when she'd called for directions to a veterinarian.

Dr. Wilson gave Cinnamon a thorough examination, which she submitted to with only a small whimper.

Dr. Wilson glanced up at Kate. "Diagnosis?" he demanded.

"Dislocated patella," she said.

"Why?"

"Common injury in this breed. Tenderness and swelling. Dislocation apparent on external exam."

Dr. Wilson nodded. "So what are we going to do?"

"Anesthetize the dog and reduce the dislocation, using the standard surgical procedure."

"Ordinarily, yes. But we don't have equipment small enough for a Pom. So?"

"Sedation via IV. Reduce the dislocation without opening the knee."

Dr. Wilson gave her a smile and a pat on the shoulder. He glanced over at Char, who was chewing on a thumbnail and immediately stopped when he addressed her. "That's what we're going to do, okay? Then we'll keep the knee immobilized for a few days. We'll improvise something for that. She'll be good as new in no time."

"Will she have to stay overnight?"

"Not if she tolerates the procedure well."

"How much will it cost?" Char had to ask, even though she hated having to do it.

Kate glanced at Char. "The charge is six hundred dollars, but we accept barter, payment plans, and major credit cards."

"Hush up, Kate," Dr. Wilson told his daughter pleasantly. "Don't worry about it, Ms. Simmons. We'll work something out. Pay what you can when you can."

"Thank you," Char said, her face burning. She'd never had a lot of money, but she'd always been able to make ends meet. It didn't make a difference that it wasn't exactly her fault she'd ended up like this; it was still humiliating. She

Cold Hands, Warm Hearts

couldn't bring herself to meet Dr. Wilson's eyes. She just took Abby's hand and led her back to the waiting room so that Dr. Wilson and Kate could get started.

Char had read every back issue of *Field and Stream* in the rack on the wall and had answered approximately 372 of Abby's questions by the time Kate came out of the back. She told them the procedure was finished and invited them to follow her back to the exam room where Cinnamon and Dr. Wilson were waiting.

"Good as new," Dr. Wilson said cheerfully when they walked in. "She tolerated the procedure just fine." Cinnamon gave a sleepy bark of disagreement, and Dr. Wilson rubbed her ears. "She'll have to wear this immobilizer until the swelling goes down," he said, "but she should be fine in a few days. Try to keep her quiet, and don't let her run around. Crate her if you have to."

He opened a manila folder on the table next to Cinnamon and pulled a sheet of paper out. "Discharge instructions. Call if she starts acting differently from usual, or if she seems to be in a lot of pain. She'll be tired this afternoon but should recover from the sedation by morning. Let me know if you have any questions." He handed the sheet of instructions to Char, who folded it and tucked it in her pocket.

"The charge is not six hundred dollars," he said with a glance at his daughter. "That's just what Kate thinks I should charge because she wants a new car." Kate grinned at him. "The charge is four hundred dollars, and you just pay as you can." He handed a written bill to Char.

"Wait a minute," Abby said. She dug into her pocket and produced two crumpled dollar bills. "We can pay a little now."

"Abby," Char said helplessly, not knowing what to say.

"It's my allowance," Abby said stubbornly. "I want to help. I don't need it right now."

Dr. Wilson glanced at Char, then twitched the money out of Abby's hand. "All right," he said. "Two dollars paid on November 15, leaving a balance of three hundred and ninety-eight dollars." He straightened out the bills, then handed them to Kate. "Please put this in the cash drawer," he said. Then he added, "Thank you," to Abby.

"Can I carry her to the car, Mom?"

"Yes," Char said, biting back the impulse to say, "Be careful." Then she remembered she'd meant to tell Dr. Wilson about the broken window she'd seen. "Oh, I should mention—we're living out on Silver Lake for the winter. Keith, the handyman who helped us get settled, says your family owns the neighboring place."

Dr. Wilson raised an eyebrow and said, "We do own a small property out there. It's pretty isolated at this time of year."

"We'll be fine," Char said, as she'd said so many times before. "I wanted to mention that there's a broken window in your house. In the cellar. You may want to have someone come out to take a look at it. It could cause some flood damage."

She explained what she'd seen. Dr. Wilson listened, then said, "Thanks. I'll send my brother along in the morning. I'll have him introduce himself to you so you know he's supposed to be there." A hesitation followed. "Don't let him bother you. He's got a thorn in his paw and isn't much company these days."

Her mama had brought her up so well, she knew it'd be impolite to ask what the thorn was, but she did anyway. Dr.

Wilson glanced over the rims of his glasses at her and said sharply, "You're not the kind who takes in strays, are you?"

"Absolutely not," Char promised. "Even Cinnamon came from a well-respected breeder."

"Good. He won't tell me what the thorn is. I just know it's there."

"You mean, don't bother inviting him in for milk and cookies?"

Dr. Wilson smiled. "Well, feel free. Just don't be surprised when he says no."

Chapter Two

*U*h-oh.

The rangy, dark-haired man boasted a two-day beard, too-long hair, and hard, intensely gray eyes that seemed disinclined to overlook normal human frailty. He wore the North Woods uniform of heavy jeans, sweatshirt, work boots, and unzipped parka, but he wore it . . . *ironically* was all Char could think. He was attractive, and she'd been a long time without a date, but . . .

Cop.

She would know that demeanor anywhere. Wary, confident, and competent. That could only mean *cop*. That knowledge trumped everything else: her dry throat, her swiftly beating heart, her sweating palms, her hormones yelling, *What would it hurt?* It would hurt, she knew. A lot.

"Hi," Char said, her fingers clenching the door frame. *Why didn't Dr. Wilson tell me his brother was a cop?* She could feel the warmth of the man's body from where she stood. She could feel the pull of attraction, dark and sweet and hypnotic. *Oh, no.* She was not attracted to a cop. Not now, not ever. No way. But especially *not now*.

Abby appeared in the hall behind her. "Who is it?" she

asked, as if it might be a friend from down the street, despite the fact that they were living in a cabin on a remote lake in northern Minnesota and didn't have any friends down the street.

"Dr. Wilson's brother," Char said. "Max. At least that's who I think it is." She smiled at the man in the doorway. *See? We've got nothing to hide.*

"Correct," the man said without returning the smile. *See?* Only a cop confirmed a statement like that. "Philip said I should check in with you first."

"Okay," Char said. "Do you want me to explain—"

"No need."

"Okay, you handle it," Char said, and she closed the door in his face. She caught the glint of surprise in Max's eyes just before she did so. A smile of satisfaction formed on her lips as she bolted the door, the *snick* of it sliding home a secondary impoliteness, like giving someone the raspberry after you've insulted him. Her mother would have been mortified.

"That was rude," Abby said.

"What was? His interrupting me and using that patronizing tone of voice? Or my shutting the door in his face?"

"Both," Abby said after careful consideration.

"Could be," Char agreed. Every instinct screamed for her to keep her distance from him. To keep her distance from any cop, but especially this one, with his flat gray eyes unwilling to overlook normal human frailty. Char was normal. She was human. She was frail. She could do the math.

Besides, shutting the door meant she was in control. Wielding a little power over her environment always made her feel stronger, and Char needed as much strength as she could get at the moment. She smiled down at her daughter.

"I'd better not catch you doing a thing like that. Aren't you dressed yet? You're going to miss clean-out-the-shed day if you don't get a move on."

With a heartfelt sigh, Abby went into the tiny bedroom to change. Char watched out the front window and made sure that Max Wilson was out of sight before she unbolted the door and stepped out of the cabin. She double-checked that the coast was clear, then grabbed her parka and walked to the detached shed that she hoped could serve as a garage. It was packed to the rafters with junk that Aunt Kay's long-deceased husband had stored and abandoned there, but Char wanted to park her car inside. Leaving the little econobox outside throughout an entire North Woods winter seemed like an excellent way to ensure it never started again.

A while later, a haphazardly dressed Abby came out to help her clean but didn't seem inclined to do much except watch the proceedings. Char didn't push. Abby was still recovering from an extremely traumatic experience. And instead of being able to bring her home and help her regain her strength in familiar surroundings, Char had to—

She shoved the self-recriminations aside and turned back to a carton of paint cans resting in a corner. The paint had turned to the consistency of sludge, so she knew it should be tossed, but there was a faded name scrawled on the side of the box, as if the paint might belong to someone else and Uncle Ned had let that person store it there. That was in character, but it also meant she might be throwing away something that didn't technically belong to her. On the other hand, she couldn't store other people's useless paint. In her mind she could hear an elderly voice quarreling with her: *Those were perfectly good cans of paint!* Uncle Ned, an inveterate pack rat, had always thought everything was perfectly good even when it was plainly not.

"Easier to ask forgiveness," she said out loud as she carried the carton to join the other discards out in front of the shed.

"What crime were you contemplating?" The male voice made her jump, but she didn't lose her grip on the box. She looked up at the man standing in front of her, hands jammed in his jeans' pockets. Smooth and silent, like a cat. *Sleek,* her mind supplied. *Well-muscled,* it offered. *Strong.*

Stop that. Her mind locked into thesaurus mode every now and then, and it tended to get stuck there for a while.

The crime? The crime.

"The crime of throwing away a couple of perfectly good cans of paint," she said equitably. "Please don't arrest me."

"Those aren't perfectly good cans of paint," Max said, scowling.

"Good," Char said, dumping the box onto the pile. "You can be my witness."

"Right," he said. "I'm getting ready to leave."

"Okay," Char said, and she turned back to go into the shed.

"I'd like to talk to you a second," Max said. Then, with a glance toward Abby, he added, "Alone."

No was the obvious answer, though she didn't really think that Max was gearing up to ask her out on a date or anything similar. He certainly didn't give that impression. But still. He was a cop, or at least he gave a very good imitation of one. Could any good come of any private conversation she might have with him? *No, I want nothing to do with you. Go away.* The words were easy enough to say. But Abby would point out that such a response was rude, and she really needed to try to be a better role model for her daughter, considering what a disastrous role model Abby's father was turning out to be. Besides, Char wanted to know what Max Wilson had on his mind. What was that old saying? Keep your friends close but your enemies closer? Not that Max was an enemy, per se.

She was doing it again. She gave Max a bright smile, said, "Sure thing," then glanced at Abby. "Abby, can you let Cinnamon out? Make sure you watch her really carefully while she's doing her business. Then go on inside. I'll be there in a minute. We'll take a little break."

"Sure," Abby said. Obviously the promise of a break appealed to her a lot more than the promise of hard work. She jumped up and walked toward the cabin. Char watched until the front door shut behind her.

"So, what's going on?" Char asked, turning back toward Max.

"It looks like someone broke in the window to get into the place. It's such a mess in there, I can't even tell if anything's missing. But it looks like whoever got in spent some time inside. They didn't vandalize the place—not that I could tell, anyway—but some burn marks on one of the bedroom floors upstairs make it look like someone built a campfire for warmth. Philip—my brother—hasn't opened the place in a couple of years, so there's no oil for the furnace, and the electricity is off. I boarded the broken window up, but that won't necessarily keep anyone out." He gave her a long, measuring look. He'd laid all the facts for her to assemble, to make of them what she would.

Char swallowed hard. The thought of squatters breaking

MORLEY LIBRARY
phone: 440 352 3383
online: www.morleylibrary.org

Title: Zippo lighters : an identification
and price guide
Author: Pope, Kristian.
Call number: 688.4 LE
Item ID: 30112101776273
Date due: 3/28/2020,23:59

Title: Cold hands, warm hearts
Author: Jacobs, Jenny, 1965-
Call number: JACOBS COLD
Item ID: 30112103514383
Date due: 3/28/2020,23:59

Title: Meat and candy
Author: Old Dominion (Musical group),
Call number: OLD DOMINION MEAT
Item ID: 30112105008061
Date due: 3/21/2020,23:59

Title: Traveller
Author: Stapleton, Chris (Musician),
Call number: STAPLETON
TRAVELLER
Item ID: 30112104935710
Date due: 3/21/2020,23:59

Total checkouts for session:4
Total checkouts:4

into the place nearest hers sent warning flares through her mind. She and Abby were so isolated out here. What would she do if they were threatened? There wasn't a phone or even a phone line in the cabin, and her cell phone didn't get reception here. She had to drive several miles for that.

"The burn marks don't look recent," he added. "I think whoever got in is long gone."

She supposed that was meant to be reassuring. She glanced over her shoulder as she heard the front door slam. Abby came out of the cabin with a wriggling Cinnamon in her arms, trying to convince the dog she couldn't do her usual running and dashing around the yard with one leg immobilized.

"Would you let my brother know if you see anything else?" he asked. "Anything that looks like it's been disturbed?" He hesitated when she didn't immediately answer, then asked, "No phone?"

She shook her head, wrapping her arms around herself. "My aunt and uncle never had a line put in."

He gave her a look out of those gray eyes, and her shoulders tensed defensively. *Doing the best I can* seemed like a really feeble excuse at the moment. He stood there for a minute, turning something over in his mind. Then he finally said, "There's a line at our place. I'll see about getting someone over tomorrow to have it tested and turned on."

"You don't need to do that," Char said through tight lips. "It'd be quite a hike to get over there if some random burglar tried to break in here."

"I was thinking about if something happened to Abby. It'd be a lot closer to your cabin than the nearest spot where you can pick up a cell signal."

There was that.

"We're fine. We'll be fine," she said. "Really. Don't worry about us."

"I'll come back tomorrow," Max said, just as if she hadn't spoken.

Well, let him. Then there'd be a working phone within a reasonable distance, and she could remove the fear of not being able to call for help from the list of things keeping her awake at night. That list was already plenty long enough.

Max climbed into his car, closing the door with a decisive *thunk*. Char watched as he swung the car around in the driveway and headed up the hill. Pennsylvania tags on the nondescript Buick. Cop car. Big-city cop car. A cold chill having nothing to do with the weather crawled up her back. What was he doing here? And, given what Dr. Wilson had said about his disposition, why was he being so helpful?

"So?" Philip asked, passing mashed potatoes to Max but hoarding the gravy boat. "What happened at the cabin?"

Kate, Max's niece, shivered, a glass of water halfway to her lips. "That place has always given me the creeps, even in the middle of summer. When I was a kid—"

"How's your feline anatomy class, dear?" interrupted Elaine, Philip's wife. She sent a sidelong glance in Philip's direction, and he surrendered the gravy boat after a brief internal struggle that played out on his face. Elaine would have made an excellent commanding officer, able to exert control over multiple developing situations at once.

Kate rolled her eyes. "Smooth change of subject, Mom. It's fine. I'm brilliant, you know."

Max grinned at his niece, who, despite knowing she'd

Cold Hands, Warm Hearts

been manipulated away from her complaint, went along with it, which was probably the best way to deal with Elaine.

"Potatoes are delicious," he said. Then he added, "Gravy too."

"Thank you," Elaine said. "How'd you do on the midterm?" she asked Kate.

"I passed with flying colors. Did you ever doubt it?"

"Of course not," Philip interjected. "When do classes start again?"

"That would be after Thanksgiving," Kate said with another exaggerated roll of her eyes. "I thought you missed me terribly when I'm gone."

"I do," Philip said. "But I'm out of practice having you here."

Max could very well see how you might "get out of practice" and become accustomed to the companionable quiet. Elaine was not a chattering woman, unlike her daughter.

"When do *you* go back?" Kate asked Max, snagging the last biscuit from the basket and slathering it with butter.

There was an awkward silence around the table that Max didn't feel like being the first one to break. Kate took in the pinched expressions on her parents' faces and said, "Oops," then took a big bite of the biscuit.

Max half expected her to push, playing the, "Hey, I'm a grown-up and have a right to know" card, but she didn't. Occasionally, she possessed a wisdom beyond her years.

"So?" Philip asked, giving Max a pointed look. "The cabin?"

"So." Max shrugged. "I checked it out."

"Checked it out or checked her out?" Kate snorted, showing that her possession of wisdom beyond her years was limited in scope.

"Kate!" That was Elaine, trying to look and sound scandalized, but he could tell by the appraising glance she gave him and the lift of one eyebrow that she was as curious as Kate.

"Well, she's really pretty," Kate said defensively. "And she's got those big brown eyes and that 'I'm completely out of my element' manner and that little ball of fluffy dog, and some guys really go for that."

Max had noticed the big brown eyes but not the "I'm completely out of my element" manner. She'd seemed perfectly able to hold her own. Maybe she only used the "I'm completely out of my element" ploy on men who were susceptible to it, like Philip. Which Philip proved by saying, "I don't like it. I don't like that she's all the way out there, alone with her kid, who has obviously just had brain surgery. She doesn't have any money. She owns a Pomeranian, for heaven's sake. How tough can she be?"

Max grunted. *Tough enough,* he thought, remembering how she'd slammed the door in his face. It intrigued him. Sure, she'd stopped to give him the time of day later but only because he'd insisted on it, and she hadn't liked it. So that intrigued him, because he wondered why. It couldn't be anything personal she objected to; they hardly knew each other. So it must be something else. He supposed it was possible she'd made him as a cop and had something to hide. Wasn't that the way?

Kate gave her father a look. "Weren't you the one who told her what a great watchdog her Pom is?"

"That, young lady, is known as having a good bedside manner. You can't insult your clients if you want to see them again."

"Sure you can," Kate said with asperity. "If you don't charge them for your services."

"Oh, for goodness sakes," Elaine put in. "Your father is entitled to run his practice in the way he sees fit. He's been doing it for twenty-five years."

"She is really pretty," Kate said meditatively, emptying the gravy boat over her potatoes.

"Kate!" That was both Philip and Elaine at the same time. Max guessed they were each objecting to different things.

"I boarded up the broken window," Max said. "I checked inside, and it looks as if you had some squatters in there. Hard to tell if anything was stolen."

"I don't know why you don't sell the place," Kate said. "We never go there anymore, and it's just a firetrap. Think of the liability."

"Nothing for you to worry about," Philip said just as Elaine chimed in, "She's right, you know."

This time it was Philip who rolled his eyes. "I don't disagree. But I don't have time to sort through that mess and get the place ready to sell. And Kate's at school all year and goes into residency in May. And you, my dear"—he gave Elaine a warm smile that made her blush a little—"cannot be spared for such mundane tasks."

Max knew that Elaine put in long hours as a therapist at a regional mental-health clinic, and though she took pleasure in looking after her family, she'd have neither interest nor desire to clean up the mess left behind by her in-laws.

That was when he became aware that everyone was looking at him.

"There," Philip said with satisfaction. "I've been worried about that girl, and this would be an excellent way to keep an eye on her."

Max knew he could protest. He could even threaten to go back to Philadelphia. He chewed his lip and considered. He didn't mind doing the housekeeping; he was at loose ends, and it would give him something to do, a purpose, no matter how mundane. But the real reason he even considered it was because of the woman who was living in the cabin next door. She was pretty, sure, but that wasn't what piqued his interest. Or, to be precise, it wasn't the only thing that did.

"What else have you got going on?"

Every ounce of experience Max possessed told him she was running from something. He wondered what. He felt the stir along his cop instincts, a stirring he hadn't felt in a long time, and in some ways he resented it. That part of his life was done; it was all over but the paperwork. Granted, following up on the cop instincts might make the winter a whole lot more interesting than previously expected. But what price would he end up paying?

Abby napped, snuggled under the covers on the daybed in the main room. Char saw no sign of the dog and took a quick look around the cabin. She found Cinnamon curled up in a nest of blankets at the foot of Abby's empty bed, where she would be comfortable but safe from Abby's restless sleep as well as her exuberant affection.

Cinnamon wagged her tail at Char's presence but didn't move from her spot, and after gently ruffling her fur, Char slipped out of the alcove to let the dog rest. In the main room, she sat down next to Abby on the daybed, remembering that she'd wanted to check the scar for signs of infection as Regina, Abby's nurse, had advised her to. The hair in the area around the scar had started to grow back in, short stubble that was almost more painful to see than the bare skin had been. How far Char and Abby had to go, the tiny, fragile hair seemed to say. They were only at the very beginning. But at least it was a beginning. How differently everything could have turned out. She touched her daughter's longer hair where her head hadn't been shaved. It felt silky and soft between her fingers, a healthy child's hair. Which Abby had been before and which she would be again.

The scar looked less angry than it had. The redness and swelling had gone down. Or maybe she was just getting used to it. You could get used to anything if you had to. Char slathered antibiotic cream on the scar every night faithfully, just as Regina had told her to, and the healing wound looked fine, to her untrained eye.

She stroked Abby's cheek, the soft roundness there the last vestige of her daughter's baby-ness. The tears welled in Char's eyes. Right now, everything seemed so tenuous and fragile, as if she was just one step from disaster, balanced on a tightrope, no net. But she hadn't always felt that way. There'd been many times since she and Theodore divorced when she'd felt intrepid and courageous and sure of herself. Sure that she would never fail Abby or herself.

In those days, even the silences seemed promising. If she didn't hear back from an editor right away, it meant her ideas were under serious consideration and an assignment was sure to follow. The silence then held the flavor of anticipation. She built fantasy worlds in the silence. Pulitzer Prizes, and the esteem of her colleagues, and fat royalty checks. The silence was different now. It mocked her, reminding her of her failings, of the dreams that had never come true.

Char went into the tiny kitchen to collect the ingredients to bake cookies, using the round dinette table in the living area to mix the dough and scoop it onto the cookie sheets. At least that was productive. At the end of the task there would be something good to eat. There weren't many jobs more satisfying than that. Besides, it made her feel competent, and even if she did her worst and failed completely, the only downside was burned bottoms on the cookies.

She'd just put the first sheet of cookies into the temperamental oven when Abby padded into the kitchen.

"Why didn't you wait for me to help?" she asked, her voice tingeing to sullen, the way it always did after a nap, when she hadn't quite woken up yet.

"I didn't know how long you'd be asleep," Char said lightly as she set the timer, not wanting to start an argument.

"I want to call Daddy."

The sentence was like a gauntlet thrown down. Tension quirked between Char's shoulder blades. Apparently Abby was spoiling for a fight, one way or the other. She knew she couldn't call Daddy, and she would be upset when Char reminded her of that fact, and she would take her unhappiness out on Char. As frustrated as Char was over the mess Theodore had left her in, financially speaking, she was far angrier over the way he'd so casually abandoned his daughter, without a single word of explanation.

Relax, Char told herself, taking a deep breath. It didn't help to fret over it, to obsess over injustices she could do

Cold Hands, Warm Hearts 33

nothing about. It was better to focus on the good things: they had a place to stay, however decrepit and remote; Abby was healing; cookies were baking. The aroma of chocolate chip cookies never failed to make everything better. She took another deep sniff of the scent and said, "I wish you could call your daddy, punkin'." The kind of thing a mother said when *no* sounded too cold and heartless but there wasn't any other answer.

Abby folded her arms across her chest and thrust out her lower lip. Char couldn't help the grin that quirked her lips at her daughter's pose. She didn't let Abby see her smile because it would just set her off; Abby hated it when she thought her feelings weren't being taken seriously enough, and Char could hardly blame her. She moved to the dinette table and started scooping teaspoonfuls of dough onto another cookie sheet.

Looking at her daughter, who'd pulled out one of the dinette chairs and perched on it, rubbing her eyes with the knuckles of one hand, Char reminded herself that, as difficult as she found the upheaval in their world, Abby must find it twice as hard, twice as bewildering. She'd grown accustomed to doing things a certain way, having certain expectations that were always met. Char had always encouraged her to call her father whenever she wanted and to spend as much time with him as he could manage—which was less than Char would have liked but was at least enough to make Abby feel her father was involved in her life and that he cared. For a long time Abby had seen him most Saturday mornings and called him frequently—such as when she and Char had a disagreement, and she wanted to convince him to take her side, or when something good had happened at school, and she wanted to share her enthusiasm with someone else in addition to Char. And sometimes Theodore would call her if it had been a few days since she'd talked to him. That always made Abby feel treasured and loved, that her father noticed her absence. Once a month, they'd arrange for a longer in-person visit, a whole weekend or even three days when Theodore could take the time off work. That was how it had gone for as long as Abby could remember.

But as this past summer turned to fall, everything had changed. The phone number Abby had memorized and used whenever she wanted to talk to Daddy had started to ring unanswered, and the messages she left went unreturned. Later, the phone calls were met with a recorded message: "This number is no longer in service." Abby knew all that. She had already cried over that—more than once. How many conversations had they had about these things and what they meant? Not that Char knew what they meant, but she did the best she could. How many more such conversations would they have to have?

"Why can't I talk to Daddy?" Abby insisted, ignoring the spoon Char offered in silent invitation for her to help with the cookies.

Apparently they were going to have to have the conversation at least one more time. Char sighed and set her spoon down, slipped into the kitchen, and flicked on the oven light to check the cookies. Just-baked cookies were always an excellent way to derail a complaint. Unfortunately, the cookies were still in their melting stage and not yet at their golden brown stage. She came back to the table and picked up the spoon.

"Daddy's not at his house," she said mildly, bracing herself.

Cold Hands, Warm Hearts

"Then where is he?" Abby demanded, as if Char might have discovered his whereabouts since the last time she'd told Abby she didn't know where he was and was willfully withholding the information from her.

When things had first started to go bad, Char used to say, "Daddy will call when he can," but then she'd felt Abby's anguish when he didn't call and nothing seemed certain or reliable anymore. So she'd changed her tack, making no promises on Theodore's behalf, which was probably wise. Now she took a deep breath. "Honey, I don't know where your daddy is. I don't know when you'll be able to see him or talk to him again. But you know he loves you and—"

"No," Abby said flatly. "He would call me if he loved me. He doesn't love me."

Char didn't know what to say. Abby certainly had a point, but she could hardly agree with it. Her silence was a mistake, though; Abby burst into tears and fled from the room, sobbing in the heartbroken way only an eight-year-old could manage. Char stared after her, thinking that she obviously should have lied, that all Abby had wanted from her was some reassurance that her Daddy did care about her. Surely a little hypocrisy in the service of that end could be forgiven. But she hadn't spoken up quickly enough, and the whole conversation couldn't have gone much worse. Had she always been such an incompetent mother, or was this a new feature of their current situation?

The kitchen timer buzzed, and she bent to take the cookies out of the oven and put them on the rack to cool. If she went in to comfort Abby, Abby would lash out at her as if it was her fault Theodore had disappeared and never called or visited her. Char was tempted to stay in the kitchen with the cookies, which smelled really good. She could almost taste the chocolate on her tongue. A cookie and a cup of coffee—what better way to bolster your spirits?

But if she didn't go in to comfort Abby, Abby would think *she* didn't care either. And she did. It was just that she hadn't yet found the right words to say to Abby. Maybe she never would. She had to try anyway. She wiped her hands on a dish towel and went to comfort her daughter.

Chapter Three

The next morning, a cold, gray Friday, Char tackled the shed again, wanting to clear it out before too much more snow flew so that she could protect the econobox from at least the worst of the winter weather. She felt a little annoyed at the effort it took just to get the car under cover. How much more work would it be to keep Abby and herself safe and secure?

Abby, whose attitude hadn't improved much over the previous day, stayed inside with a book. Char didn't actively protest this arrangement; she was enough of a coward that she preferred not having to deal with her daughter at all when she was in this mood. An equally sullen Cinnamon actually growled at Char when she tried to pat her on her way out to the shed, an incident that made Char even gladder that she had work to do with at least one closed door between her and them. Apparently the immobilizer was uncomfortable, so Char warned Abby to be extra careful with the dog, then authorized Abby to give her an extra treat. She set out cookies for Abby and welcomed the chance to escape to the solitude of the shed.

Overnight, the weather had turned colder, no longer in

the tolerable twenties and thirties but much harsher than that. The pale sun shed watery light. The day actually *looked* cold, and it wasn't even snowing. She pulled open one of the two broad doors that led into the shed and found the interior even more cheerless than the exterior. The shed wasn't wired for electricity, but she'd brought a flashlight. Now she turned it on, shedding a little illumination into the darkest of the corners.

She kept the door open for the added light. Even though she worked hard inside the garage, she had to stay bundled up against the bitter bite of the wind. The thick parka and gloves she wore made it twice as hard to do the work. How did people get anything done in this climate? She'd have suspected they hid inside their houses from the end of September to May, but she knew better; she'd seen all manner of equipment, from skis to snowmobiles, that suggested some people actually chose to pursue outdoor activities during the winter months.

As she added to the pile growing taller outside the door, she wondered how she'd get all of the discards to the dump. Maybe Keith, the handyman, with his enormous pickup truck, could help her. She'd call him and find out. Surely she wasn't the sole person in the entire state whose only vehicle was a sensible, energy-efficient, four-door passenger car that got excellent gas mileage. Other people must need help hauling things around, right?

She heard the sound of tires crunching on the snow-packed driveway and ducked out of the shed in time to see Max's Buick nosing down the hill. He'd promised he'd be back. Great. A man who kept his promises, and he was a *cop*.

She stood by the open door, hands on her hips, as he parked and got out of the car. This was her property, so why did it seem as if he owned the place? Did they teach that in the police academy?

"Back again," she said, and she bit down hard on her tongue as he slammed the car door shut and came her way. Oh, Lord, he looked just as good as she remembered. Though not any less like a cop.

She took an involuntary step back, an automatic self-preservation instinct kicking in. She wished she'd had that instinct back in the day—or at least had listened to it. Then she wouldn't have gotten tangled up with Theodore Bainbridge in the first place. Look where she'd ended up because of that. Although of course she wouldn't have given up Abby for anything, so being tangled up with Theodore hadn't been *all* bad. Just *mostly* bad.

She straightened out her line of thinking. She hadn't listened to her *he's bad news* instincts then. But she'd listen to them now and keep her distance from this man. She'd be polite, so as not to antagonize him or arouse his suspicions—she knew that her particular situation was already suspicious enough—but she must under no circumstances let him pry or snoop or get close enough to her to make a mess of everything.

She realized he'd been standing there for a while looking at her, and she wondered if he'd said something she hadn't paid attention to and if he was waiting for her to respond.

"What?" she said uncertainly, and then he snapped to attention, and she realized he'd just been looking at her too, as if she was easy on the eyes, so to speak. She felt herself blush. *Great. Two idiots in the same vicinity.* What were the odds this was going to work out all right?

He said, "I'm going to check things out at the cabin today. I stopped by the hardware store to pick up a few things.

I want to get the phone and electricity turned on and the heater serviced and running."

"Uh-huh," Char said. He hadn't been this chatty before. Why was he telling her all this? Why was he *doing* all this? What was going on?

"Monday a Dumpster will be delivered, so I can start cleaning the place out," he went on, almost as if he'd carefully memorized his lines and had been warned not to try to be extemporaneous. She could almost imagine Dr. Wilson saying to him, *Now you have to be polite and tell her what's going on so she doesn't get scared off with all of the comings and goings.* Yet somehow she thought there was more to this volubility than Dr. Wilson's warning his brother to be nice.

As she waited, Max shifted—uncomfortable with what he was saying, or just plain cold?—and added, "Philip and I agreed to sell the place in the spring, and it's going to take a lot of work to get it ready."

"Uh-huh," Char said again, her suspicions on high alert. Not that she disbelieved him exactly. But he was telling her this for a reason, she was pretty sure, and that meant it involved her somehow. That thought went through her like a cold shiver. *Oh, no.* She would not get involved. Not if it required proximity to a cop. Especially this one. Why couldn't he be old, fat, bald—and married?

"I told Philip I'd spend some time up here getting the place presentable. Ma was a pack rat, and so was Dad. So there's a lot to do." Now he smiled, which didn't seem fair, because he already had the full authority and sway of the justice system behind him. He didn't need that smile too.

"Uh-huh," Char said yet again, stunned into silence. It didn't happen very often, but occasionally a situation presented itself where she had no idea what to say. Or do. Or even think. This was one of those situations.

"And since I'm going to need some help . . ." Here the smile became a little sheepish, as if he'd already gauged her potential reaction to what he intended to say.

Char's spine stiffened. She knew exactly what he intended to say.

"We thought maybe we could hire you. Can you work a couple of hours a day? You can bring Abby." He said this in a rush that might have made her feel a little sorry for him—she doubted he often found himself in situations where he felt uncertain or worried about being rebuffed and didn't know quite how to handle himself—but she wasn't capable of entertaining any emotion except something she was pretty sure was muted shock. Philip and Max Wilson were offering her a job? How was she supposed to feel about that? The numbness loosened a little, and her pride stung first.

"Did Dr. Wilson mention I owe him some money?" Her question had a little more bite to it than was probably absolutely necessary, but there it was. What would happen if she told Max what she was thinking right now? She could take care of herself and Abby. She'd managed so far, hadn't she, and against some pretty overwhelming odds? On the other hand, she owed Dr. Wilson the money, and it wasn't as if anyone else was knocking on her door offering to pay her for her time and trouble.

She eyed Max. Was this simply an excuse for him to keep tabs on her? Maybe he was somehow involved in the investigation that had ended up with Theodore's disappearing. Was that possible? And if so, maybe it would help if she kept an eye on *him*. Was keeping an eye on a cop a good idea or a bad one?

"He mentioned that you seemed to be a little short of cash. But the status of Philip's accounts-receivable is not the reason we're hoping you'll help out."

Was that a long-winded way of saying, *We know you're broke, but there's a way to turn this into a win-win situation for everyone*? Which was how Theodore would have put it. She guessed she appreciated Max's delicacy of speech.

"It's okay," she said, making a decision. She'd be under a lot more suspicion by refusing to have anything to do with Max and his brother than if she went along with the plan. Besides, heaven knew it was no hardship to keep an eye on Max. She'd simply have to keep her guard up. She gave him a glance. *Way* up. "You have evidence that I know how to throw things away." She gestured at the pile of discards from the shed. "And evidence that I'm not independently wealthy. Plus, I happen to live next door. So I can see where you got the idea to ask me. How much are you offering?" she asked with a grin. *See? Nothing suspicious about me*. Guileless, open, aboveboard. *I have no secrets,* she projected mentally, in case he was susceptible to psychic influences. She strongly doubted he was susceptible to anything but facts and logic, but you never knew.

Max narrowed his eyes at her; apparently her innocent act wasn't that convincing. She backed off on the grin a little bit, then stamped her feet in her boots to show that her toes were freezing while they debated the details. After a moment, he named an hourly figure that seemed reasonable.

"Okay," she said with a quick nod. She refrained from asking if he'd pay Abby the same rate. She suspected Abby would hinder as much as help, so that was probably a wash. "Let me finish up here." She motioned to the interior of the shed. "Abby and I can start Monday."

"Okay," Max said. He hesitated and added, "I'd help with the shed, but I have to meet those workers."

"No problem," Char said firmly. She did not need to work side by side with him under any circumstances but particularly not in the close quarters of the shed. "And I appreciate the job."

"Okay."

Still, he stayed where he was standing. What was he doing? Was he trying to give her a heart attack, just standing there and waiting for her to confess all?

"Something else you wanted?" Char asked, working hard to keep her voice mild. He was making her very nervous.

"No," he said hastily, ducking into his Buick. She winced in sympathy as he knocked his head against the frame. "See you on Monday," he called out before closing the car door behind him.

He backed and turned the Buick up the hill. She raised a hand and saw him wave back. *Great.* She was going to be friends with a cop. Just what she'd always wanted.

With a spurt of energy sourced almost entirely by extreme anxiety, Char finished cleaning out the shed that morning, pulled the econobox inside, and breathed a sigh of relief when the shed doors clicked shut behind it with a few inches to spare. She headed into the cabin to take a much-needed shower and, if she was lucky and Abby didn't badger her too much, put her feet up for a few minutes.

"Hey, punkin'," she called, pulling off her parka and hanging it on the coat tree, then tossing gloves and hat into the basket on the shelf near the door. She bent to pull her boots off, then peeled her socks off, rubbed some circulation back into her toes, and walked into the main room.

She spotted Abby there, brushing Cinnamon's coat. Char held back the urge to tell her to be careful of Cinnamon's hurt leg. Abby knew Cinnamon had been hurt. She didn't need to be told again. Char realized she'd been holding back a lot of comments lately. Abby was growing up—and maybe so was Char. Or maybe she was just learning that she couldn't control everything. Although possibly that was the same as growing up? Or at least closely related.

Abby worked with steady concentration as the dog wriggled in her lap and tried to escape. She pulled a treat from her pocket, and that settled Cinnamon down for a few seconds of eager crunching and gulping.

"You're doing a good job," Char said, not commenting about the dog fur on the daybed. Abby had brought over the trash can, but not all of the fur was making its way in there. Still, Char reminded herself, Abby was trying, and just because she herself could do it more neatly didn't mean she should.

"She was getting matted," Abby explained. "I could tell when I petted her."

"Good job," Char said again. She lowered herself to the armchair in the corner, then scooted it a little nearer the heat register so she could defrost a little faster. "That shows a lot of initiative."

"What's that?"

"Taking charge. Doing what needs to be done without having to be told."

"Oh. You show initiative too," Abby complimented her generously, stretching the word out a few more syllables than it actually contained.

Char gave her a startled glance. She'd thought she'd defined the word correctly, but she certainly didn't feel as if she'd showed much initiative lately. She reacted to events, sometimes more effectively than at other times, but she wouldn't call running around putting out one fire after another, taking charge of anything.

"Thanks, punkin'," she said anyway, not sharing her doubts. Maybe she should give herself a little more credit. Or maybe Abby was just softening her up because she wanted something. Cynical, yes, but every mother was well aware of her child's ability to manipulate others to produce a desired outcome.

Abby ran the brush down Cinnamon's back one last time, then patted the dog on the head and released her. Cinnamon shook her coat as if she'd gotten caught in a rainstorm and limped away from Abby and her dreaded brush as quickly as she could go. She crawled under the bed in the alcove, apparently assuming Abby couldn't reach her there. But a Pomeranian was no match for a determined eight-year-old, Char thought. *She* was hardly a match for a determined eight-year-old.

"You work hard, Mama," Abby said, getting to her feet and leaving the brush and drifts of fur all over the daybed. "We both do."

"Uh-huh," Char said, now no longer suspecting she was being softened up for something but knowing it. She felt it was fair, at this point, to say, "Don't forget to put the brush away. And see where some of Cinnamon's fur didn't make it into the trash?"

Abby gave a mutinous look—after all the effort she'd gone to, her mom insisted on being picky—but stomped away with the brush without saying anything, then came back and picked up most of the fur and threw it away. "There," she said firmly, as if daring Char to demand greater perfection, but Char was willing to settle for mediocrity and said only, "Thanks, punkin'."

"So can I watch some TV?" Abby asked. Then, in case Char had missed the connection, she added, "Seeing as I worked so hard, I should get a reward, right?"

Char looked around the room. She'd felt as if there was something missing from the space, and now she knew what it was. "I don't see a television here," she said.

Abby's face fell as she darted a glance around the room too. "No television!" she exclaimed, then ran into the bedroom alcove. Char could hear her opening the closet doors, as if the television might be hidden there.

"No TV!" Abby said, coming back into the room and collapsing on the daybed and making tufts of fur fly. She sneezed. "I can't believe we're stuck here with no TV!"

"The reception's probably really bad anyway," Char consoled her.

"I bet there's not even cable," Abby agreed glumly. "What am I supposed to do with myself?" For a moment, Char glimpsed the drama-prone teenager Abby was going to become and hid a smile. At least Abby was going to have that chance. When she thought about how close they'd come . . .

"Read a book," Char suggested. "Write a story. Draw a picture. Help me fix lunch." She had a selection of less-pleasing activities on tap if Abby balked. But Abby didn't, being mostly good-natured and willing to go along on this adventure.

"Lunch," Abby decided, scrambling to her feet, then coming over to help haul Char out of her chair.

Soon, Char was setting out plates of scrambled eggs and pancakes. Per Abby's request, which Char indulged hap-

Cold Hands, Warm Hearts 47

pily enough, lunch looked a lot like breakfast. Char forked eggs and pancakes into her mouth, then went to take a shower as Abby finished her lunch.

When she returned to the kitchen after she'd dressed, she noted that Abby's initiative had not spread to washing the dishes, although she had put her plate down for Cinnamon to lick. They'd already had a conversation about how that didn't count as dishwashing, and Char didn't repeat it. She wiped the bottle of sticky syrup and put it away, handed Abby a dish towel, and had the kitchen back in shape in just a few minutes. If only the other areas of her life would be so susceptible to order.

"I need to call Deanna," Char told Abby. "And we have to get a few things from the grocery store."

Abby's face brightened at that. A few weeks ago, Char knew, Abby wouldn't have considered a trip to the grocery store a treat, but she did now. Abby dried the last plate and put it into the cabinet. "Ready," she said, which wasn't exactly true, because there were boots and parkas to be donned and mittens and gloves to be found, but it was only a few minutes later when the two of them headed outside.

"You got the garage done," Abby said as Char hauled open the double doors to reveal the shed's newly neatened interior, the econobox carefully squeezed inside. "Excellent initiative, Mom."

"Don't be a brat," Char said. Abby gave her a grin and followed her into the shed. Char was thankful that Abby's humor had improved to her normal disposition, where they could tease each other a little. She felt her own disposition brighten in response.

"The car should be unlocked," Char said when Abby didn't immediately reach for the door. One thing about being this far from civilization was that she wasn't really worried about random thieves breaking into her car.

Abby climbed into the backseat with a sticker book she'd brought home from the hospital to entertain her during the drive. Already she'd learned that a trip to the grocery store wasn't a quick jaunt but an expedition. The newness of the experience would undoubtedly wear off, but Char was thankful for Abby's playing along just now.

She carefully backed the car out of the shed, then paused and remembered to turn on her cell phone, setting it on the seat next to her so she could see the screen. She drove up the driveway and onto the main county road heading toward Grand Rapids. The nearest city of any size—"Not Grand Rapids, Michigan," Keith, the handyman, had emphasized, "but Grand Rapids, Minnesota." She'd carefully memorized the roads they'd taken the day they'd gone there to lay in supplies, and she had a map in the door pocket by her left ankle.

As she drove, occasionally she glanced at the cell phone to see if it showed any sign of service yet. They'd been on the road for twenty minutes before Char thought the signal was strong enough to prevent a dropped call.

Even though there was no traffic, she pulled onto the shoulder of the road before picking up the phone. Being Abby's mother meant acting like a role model even on those occasions when it didn't seem vitally necessary. The icon on the phone's screen told her she had messages, but talking to Deanna was her priority, so she called her friend's number first.

"Char? Oh, my gosh, I'm so glad you called!" Deanna exclaimed, and her friend's warm voice eased some of the tension from Char's body. Deanna had been her friend

Cold Hands, Warm Hearts 49

since college, when the dorm lottery had turned them into roommates. They'd negotiated the challenges of college life together, first by chance, then by choice, and they'd kept making that choice in the years since graduation. Deanna had been there through it all, her life sometimes paralleling Char's—graduation, first awful job at an insurance company—and sometimes diverging—grassroots activism with a call-center job to pay the bills, for Deanna, freelancing with its ups and downs for Char.

Deanna had remained single, though she often had a boyfriend somewhere in the background, usually a man she'd met saving the wetlands or protesting a ban on panhandling as an infringement of free speech. Char had married and had Abby and wrote about rodeo clowns, performance artists, and other interesting people. They'd gotten dogs around the same time—Deanna an Akita mix from a shelter, and Char a Pomeranian from a carefully chosen breeder after Abby had fallen in love with the breed as a tiny girl playing with a neighbor's dog.

Deanna's had been the shoulder Char cried on when her marriage to Theodore ended. Char's shoulder had been used a few times by Deanna; the limited duration of her relationships did not reduce their intensity or her sorrow over their ending.

"How is everything?" Deanna asked. "I can't believe I haven't talked to you in this long."

"It's been fine. Better than I expected," Char said, hearing the false heartiness in her own voice and disliking it. She hoped Abby didn't notice. "How are things back home?" she asked, trying to find her regular voice.

"Um," Deanna said, and Char froze. Deanna never told an outright lie, not even in the service of small talk or social lubrication, so she sometimes didn't answer at all if she decided that was the more appealing option. "You'll be glad to know you finally got that check from that magazine," she said in a rush.

Despite the lack of specifics, Char knew what Deanna was talking about. "Thank goodness," Char said. "That should have arrived months ago." Deanna had a key to Char's post office box and was depositing checks into her account and letting her know what arrived in the mail. Char knew the process wasn't exactly leaving no trail behind, but she wasn't like Theodore: she didn't know all the details of how to hide out from trouble without anyone finding you. And she didn't have a ready stash of cash to use so that she didn't have to draw on her bank account. She was just doing the best she could, and she hoped that if Theodore—or his friends or enemies—ever tracked her to Grand Rapids, they didn't narrow it down further.

It was a fine line between being safe and being paranoid.

"How much was the check for?" she asked, wanting to make sure the accounts-payable clerk had gotten it right despite the comedy of errors that had kept the check out of Char's hands for this long.

Deanna told her. The amount matched what her invoice had said—a correspondence that wasn't always the case, in Char's experience. The few hundred dollars wasn't much, really, but it made Char feel rich. Amazing how a little experience could alter one's perspective. With some funds in the bank, now she could go to the grocery store with a clear conscience.

"Thanks, Deanna," she said, her gratitude as much for the unnamed accounts-payable clerk as for the favor her friend was doing her.

"I deposited it yesterday," Deanna added. There was a pause, and Char could hear Deanna's reluctance to say the next thing. She could also hear her fidgeting—always a bad sign. Char held her breath.

"Look, Char. A sheriff's deputy stopped by my place this morning."

"What?" Char demanded. She knew that long years of experience with Theodore had made her especially jumpy, and that was why she was extrasensitive to cops, like Max Wilson. But she hadn't realized they were really after her. She gripped the phone tighter to her ear. First Max, with his oh-so-casual job offer, a subtle way of keeping an eye on her. Now sheriff's deputies—or at least *a* sheriff's deputy—visiting her best friend. Cops everywhere. What was that about? What did they want from her? She didn't have anything, not for anyone, which was why she was staying away from civilization as much as possible.

"He wanted to know if I knew where you were. They've been trying to find you."

Char's stomach turned over. *Trying to find her?*

"But, you know, someone else is living at your last known address, your landline phone's been disconnected, and you're not returning messages left on your cell phone."

"My cell doesn't work up here," Char interjected, her voice shaking. "And there aren't any landlines in the cabin." She forced herself to stop babbling before Abby cued into her alarm. She hadn't done anything wrong. She'd been stupid and married a troubled man and hadn't protected herself as well as she could or should have. But stupid wasn't against the law.

"Peter thought maybe they had someone watching the

post office box and then followed me home." Peter was Deanna's latest love.

"What?" Char demanded again. "That's crazy." But her palms started to sweat. It wasn't crazy—not if Theodore had drawn her into one of his messes again. However, it was a lot more likely that if they'd had Theodore under investigation, they'd learned a few things about Char, too, like who her best friend was. That was a simpler, more believable explanation.

"Char, how bad is it?" Deanna asked briskly. Char's friend wasn't immune to legal difficulties herself and was good buddies with any number of bail bondsmen, owing to her occasionally too-enthusiastic protests at city council meetings. "I mean, have you been sued? Is someone trying to serve you? What's going on?"

"I don't know, Deanna," Char said, swallowing hard. Her mind worked furiously. Maybe it didn't have anything to do with Theodore. Maybe it was something to do with her. But what? "I worked out a plan with the credit card company, so they wouldn't be suing me," she said. "And I just spent my last dime on the first installment on the Mayo Clinic bill. I haven't paid off the Lawrence Memorial Hospital bill yet, but I put a big chunk down—you know that; you sold everything for me." Char realized she was babbling again and stopped to catch her breath, pressing a palm against her heart. She hadn't been able to pay everyone in full yet, but she thought she'd worked out suitable arrangements. Had she missed a creditor?

"What did you tell the deputy?" she asked Deanna.

"Mom?" Abby asked from the backseat, leaning forward in alarm. Char reached back with a soothing hand

and said, "It's okay, sweetie. Just something Deanna and I need to talk about."

"I didn't tell him anything," Deanna said, her indignation carrying clearly across the miles. "You think I'm gonna help The Man?"

"Sorry," Char said, rolling her eyes. Deanna was even more paranoid about cops than Char was.

"I told him I had your cell phone number—I figure they've got that too, how hard could it be?—but I didn't have your new address yet."

That was true. Char hadn't been sure of the exact address of the cabin until she'd moved up here. She hadn't had a chance to tell Deanna what it was. Now she had the chance but didn't take it. What Deanna didn't know couldn't hurt either of them or be intercepted by any wiretaps that happened to be in place.

The phone slipped in her hand. She could hardly believe she'd had a thought like that, and yet it was possible.

Anything is possible, she reminded herself. Happily ever after was possible. Why not focus on that?

"Okay," Char said. "I'll check and see if they left a message that tells me anything. Thanks, Deanna."

"No problem," her friend said. "If you need the name of a lawyer, let me know."

That was not as reassuring as Deanna probably meant it to be. "Will do," Char said.

"Other than that," Deanna said dryly, "nothing much is happening here. Abby doing okay?"

"She's doing great. Healing just fine and enjoying our adventure."

In the rearview mirror, Char could see Abby perk up at

that, knowing she was being talked about. She poked her chin over the back of the seat. "Let me talk to Dee!"

Deanna heard the demand and chuckled, and Char handed over the phone so Abby could go into dramatic detail about what had happened to her in the last few weeks.

Char cut her off after a few minutes and said to Deanna, "Thanks. She got your cards, and she loves the stuffed wolf you sent."

"Dakota," Abby, shamelessly eavesdropping, reminded her.

"Right. She calls it Dakota," she informed Deanna.

"What else would you call a stuffed wolf?" Deanna asked. "You okay for money? I don't have a lot to spare this month, but I could send you some—"

"That's okay," Char interrupted. If possible, Deanna had even less than Char did, but she was always willing to share it. "I have a job," she added, explaining what Philip and Max Wilson had asked her to do.

Deanna didn't comment on the comedown from the successes she'd had earlier in her career and the indignity of doing scut work for a great deal less money than she was used to earning.

"Better than nothing," Deanna said prosaically. "Is he cute?"

"Who?"

"This guy. Max. Your voice changed when you said his name."

"It wasn't affection," Char said. "Although he did try to be nicer today."

"Ah. You already have a history with this guy."

"I've only met him twice," Char said, though she knew

Cold Hands, Warm Hearts 55

that didn't mean anything. With some men, it didn't take much effort to have a history. Others you could encounter on a daily basis for a year and not really be affected by it.

"And he's trying to be nicer? What does that mean?"

"Nothing," Char said, wishing she would be more careful about what she said and how she said it.

"Maybe his heart was broken as a young man by a woman with corkscrew curls, so he was wary of you on your first meeting," Deanna mused. "Then you stunned him with your warm and generous nature, and he immediately warmed to you—moth to flame." For someone as romantic as Deanna, she wasn't very imaginative.

"I don't have a kind and generous nature," Char pointed out.

"You do too. You just don't like people to know about it. Listen, gotta run, but let me know if I can do anything."

"Thanks," Char said. "Take care."

"You too."

Char hung up the phone and stared at it for a minute. She was glad some money had finally come in, but that relief was cancelled by the anxiety she had over the news that Deanna had talked to a sheriff's deputy, and that he, or one like him, was trying to reach Char. She had a stomachache just thinking about it.

She took a deep breath and steadied herself. She could do it. She could deal with whatever came. She always had. Always. This time would be no different.

"Hey, punkin'," she said, turning in her seat to look at Abby in the backseat. "I have to check my cell phone messages, and then we'll go to the grocery store."

Abby gave an exaggerated sigh to show what she thought of the delay and snapped open her sticker book again.

Someday she would outgrow sticker books and the delights of breakfast for lunch, and what would Char do then to assuage her impatience with her mother's many failings?

I haven't failed, Char reminded herself, squelching the little voice that added, *yet.* She listened to a couple of messages from acquaintances and colleagues who hadn't heard about her current situation. She opened the notebook she always kept in the car, scrabbled in the glove compartment for a pen, and jotted down names and numbers so she could call them back. None of them was actually offering projects or payment of any kind, so returning the phone calls wasn't urgent. Then she came to a series of messages from a Detective Wojociewski—"Ask for Wojo"— requesting that she call him back. He gave no indication of the nature of the matter he wished to discuss with her, just that it moved from "important" to "urgent" to "vital" in the course of the messages he'd left her.

Her hands shook as she jotted down the call-back number, then methodically deleted the messages so she wouldn't accidentally hear them again. They'd made her feel sick enough the first time through.

She took another deep breath. If she called Detective Wojo from her cell, would they—the police—be able to trace the signal and find her? Then what? What if Theodore had started telling his lies to get out of trouble? She couldn't get drawn into his mess. She had to protect Abby. What would happen if she got caught up in some sort of legal trouble because of Theodore? Abby was still in a fragile state, unable to bear much more upset. What would happen to her if Char got tangled up with the kinds of trouble Theodore attracted?

Not to mention that Char might need a lawyer to get out

of whatever the trouble was. Those kinds of lawyers didn't come cheap, and she didn't have the money for one.

But if she ducked the cops, what would happen? She knew from experience that the more you resisted, the more they pushed. Her stomach roiled with nausea. Why did she have to keep paying for her mistake of falling for Theodore? She'd learned the lesson, she'd tried to solve the problem, she'd done her best to be grown-up and fair and mature about the situation, to be amicable for Abby's sake. . . .

Char tapped the cell phone against her teeth as she thought. Finally, she shrugged. She didn't have to decide what to do right now. She could think about it. Surely she had a little time to think. Maybe get some advice. But from whom?

She turned off the phone and tossed it aside. She'd worry about it later. Now she had groceries to buy. She glanced into the rearview mirror before merging back onto the road and saw that Abby had fallen asleep. She was still easily tired, but Char knew she was getting better. Just a little more time and she'd be as good as new. Char would do whatever it took to give her that little bit of time.

Char pulled her attention back to the road. As she drove, another light snow began to fall, accumulating in ghostly white patches on the street. The road ground by, mile after mile, reminding Char how remote they were from civilization. The snow started falling faster, and Char gripped the wheel tighter. She willed herself to relax, but will didn't seem strong enough to overcome instinct.

What did the police want, and how could she find out without getting tangled up in more trouble than she could handle?

Chapter Four

Max had tried to ignore the itch as long as he could, but finally, after a snappish exchange with his brother, provoked by restless irritation, he couldn't ignore it any longer. He picked up the phone and called a friend of his in the Philadelphia field office and told him what he knew and what he wanted to find out.

It wasn't Max's friend who called him back half an hour later. It was Max's boss. A bad sign. Or a good one, depending on how you looked at it.

"I thought you were staying out of trouble," Abe Silverstein said genially.

"So did I. Apparently I landed something of interest."

"Some*one* of interest," Abe corrected.

And she'd seemed like such a nice person.

"What is it?"

"The Kansas City field office has been looking at her husband—ex-husband, I should say—on a variety of matters. He's a lawyer, in tight with some criminal interests there. Trouble is, he's gone missing."

"And?"

"And the special agent in charge down there wants to ask him a few questions."

"Not good. What's his ex-wife got to do with it?"

"She's missing too. There's a question of why and what she might know."

"She's not missing anymore," Max said.

"No. And she shouldn't have been so hard to find, considering. She's been out of the picture for a while, probably since she figured out what kind of man she got hooked up with. But they have a daughter and a civilized visitation arrangement. According to sources."

"And you think—what do you think?"

"I think it would be an excellent idea for you to keep an eye on her."

"I'm on leave."

"I can always cancel it and bring you back."

"I'm not sure I'm coming back," Max reminded him.

"You may not be sure, but I am. You're a cop, Max. What are you gonna do, start selling cars?"

"I might."

Abe's snort of derision clarified what he thought of that.

"Consider it a way of easing back into the harness. You're not involved with her, are you?" This last sentence came out in a suspicious snap.

"I've known her for about twelve minutes."

"That's not an answer, Max."

"No, I'm not involved with her."

"All right, then. Don't be. We're not sure what we've got there. You have a reasonable way of executing surveillance?"

He had a perfect way. He just wished he didn't. If he

could get out of this, he would. He used to be a good cop, but . . .

"Yeah," he said. "I've got an excellent way to keep an eye on her."

Monday morning the sunlight was a pale lemon but still a welcome change from the iron gray skies of the last few days. They'd spent most of the weekend indoors, doing schoolwork. Char had assured Abby's teachers that she'd homeschool Abby during the weeks following her recovery—not mentioning the specific details regarding the disaster they were dealing with—and had promised to make sure Abby wouldn't be behind the rest of the class when she returned to school.

"We've got a job to do," Char said to her daughter, peering into the bedroom alcove to see Abby's owlish eyes blinking at her. Only her nose and her eyes were visible above the comforter. "Up and at 'em," she called out with more cheerfulness than she felt. She wasn't a morning person, and she fully sympathized with Abby's reluctance to roll out of bed.

"Don't want to," Abby said, pulling the covers all the way over her head.

"Hey! I need my assistant ready in fifteen minutes," Char said.

Abby groaned, then seemed to think about it for a minute, because she peeked out from under the covers.

"Are you going to pay me?" she asked.

"Will you stop complaining if I do?"

"Yes," Abby said, throwing the covers back to prove it, although she didn't go to the extreme of actually getting out of bed.

"Okay." Nothing wrong with a little bribery. Char herself always responded better to rewards than to threats. "I'll give you fifty cents an hour for helping me throw stuff away."

"Seventy-five," Abby said, scrambling out of bed.

Char rolled her eyes. Where had she learned her negotiating tactics? "All right, seventy-five cents. But you'd better produce. No slacking off just because you're bored."

Abby paused in the act of opening dresser drawers and gathering up her clothes. "This is in addition to my allowance, right?" she asked suspiciously.

"Yes," Char laughed. "I should hire you as my agent. You're a pretty tough negotiator."

"Daddy used to say, 'Always ask for more,'" Abby said, which Char agreed sounded just like the man she'd married. If only she'd taken it as the warning sign it was.

She found the dog on the daybed and remembered she was supposed to check Cinny's knee. She plopped the dog onto her lap, but the minute she touched the immobilizer, Cinnamon scrambled away.

"Hold it, Cinny," Char said, hauling the dog back onto her lap. "I've got to follow Dr. Wilson's advice." While she still thought of the vet as *Dr.* Wilson, she couldn't bring herself to think of his brother as anything but Max. Why was that? Probably because she felt attracted to him. It certainly wasn't because she wanted to be his friend. Finally, she managed to undo the immobilizer. Cinnamon wriggled free of the restraint and bounded across the floor, testing out her newfound freedom.

"No residual tenderness, I guess," Char said dryly, watching Cinnamon find a comfortable spot on the carpet near the window to curl up and start licking her affected leg.

"Why is she doing that?" Abby asked. She was brushing her teeth, which Char had repeatedly reminded her was supposed to be done in the bathroom. Abby always complained that the bathroom was boring.

"It probably itches," Char said. "And it probably feels and smells a little different from usual, so she's grooming herself to make it feel more normal."

"Weird," Abby said, and she disappeared into the bathroom. She reappeared a few minutes later, fully dressed, although what was left of her hair was a mess. Char told her to get a brush.

"No!" Abby said. "I already brushed it."

"You did not," Char said mildly, herding Abby back into the bathroom. Though she tried to be as gentle as possible, the hair-brushing task was not accomplished without tears. She forbore to point out that Cinnamon handled being groomed better than Abby did.

Once they'd dressed and let Cinnamon out for her morning exercise—"Why do you call it exercise?" Abby demanded. "She's pooping!"—they hiked over to the Wilson house. Earlier, Char had heard Max's car on the road above the cabin and assumed he'd be there, ready to show them what needed to be done. She knocked on the front door, which fell open at her touch.

"Spooky," Abby said with a grin, and she made a *Twilight Zone* sound.

Char didn't need to encourage that, considering how isolated they were going to be out here this winter, so she ignored the commentary. "Max?" she called, poking her head in the front door.

"Up here," he called, sounding like an ordinary guy and not her worst nightmare. Didn't she have enough cops wanting to talk to her? Why was she cultivating a friendship with this one?

"I left the door open for you," he added, as if that weren't self-evident. "Has the Dumpster come yet?"

"Nope," Char said, walking into the house with Abby and shutting the door behind them. She stomped her snowy boots on the mat laid out near the front door and gestured for Abby to do the same. But Abby was already trailing through the living room, openmouthed.

It was quite a sight. Stacks of boxes, most sealed shut with yellowing tape, towered haphazardly to the ceiling. Pile after pile of newspapers and magazines tilted precariously against one another. Char made out a small table half-buried under mounds of ancient junk mail, and two ladder-back chairs piled with brown paper bags.

The interior of the cabin, already dark from lack of lighting, was made gloomier by the encompassing piles and the awkward, dark shadows they threw. The piles blocked any light from entering the windows. She wasn't sure she wanted to stay.

"Wow," she said, feeling awe if not admiration. "I thought my mother was a pack rat."

An aisle big enough for one person led, mazelike, through the collection of trash, though she suspected Max's mother had considered it an abundance of treasures. A break in the accumulated piles gave Char a hint as to where to find the stairs. She waded through the opening and headed up them, not surprised to see the steps lined with stacks of books. Abby, busy staring in astonishment at all there was to behold, trailed slowly behind her.

"No wonder you need some help," Char called out as she accidentally dislodged a pile of books and watched helplessly as they clattered to the bottom of the staircase, narrowly missing Abby's ankles as they tumbled by.

"No kidding," Max said once the clatter had subsided.

Using something akin to echolocation, Char located Max in a bedroom at the near end of the upstairs hall. As she worked out later, the house was built on a simple plan: the main floor consisted of a large living room separated from a kitchen by a half wall; a lean-to bathroom had been added to the kitchen; upstairs, a switchback staircase led to a narrow hallway; and two small rooms with sloping ceilings branched from each side of the hallway, tucked under the eaves.

Char found Max on his hands and knees, using an electronic device to prod at an outlet. A big battery-operated lantern shed light on his work area. When she entered the room, he rocked back on his heels and sighed. "I'm supposed to be testing the wiring so we don't end up with a fire when the electricity comes back on. For all I know, mice have made lunch of all the interior wiring."

"And that little thing is supposed to help you test the safety of the outlets?"

"Yeah." He raked a hand through his dark hair. "But I'll be darned if I can figure out how to use it."

"That means you're not an electrician," Char said, a little disappointed. Wouldn't it be nice to find out she was wrong about his being a cop and he turned out to be a tradesman instead?

"No," Max said, tossing the tool into a metal toolbox by his side. "I'm a cop."

Char took an unintentional step back. She'd known it, but here was the confirmation. *Drat.* Not that she had anything against cops as a general rule. Just that her relation-

Cold Hands, Warm Hearts

ship to Theodore had taught her that, since the cops never had reason to believe a word he was saying, they never had reason to believe a word she was saying either. She could hardly blame them, but she always wanted to point out that she'd divorced Theodore when she'd realized what he was. If *they* knew so much, maybe one of them could have given her a clue before she'd gone and tied the knot. But of course she'd never said any of that, just gritted her teeth when they said, "Of course, Mrs. Bainbridge. Do you have any evidence to back up that statement?" But how could you prove that you didn't know someone's business associates, that you didn't know how he'd made his money, that you didn't know where the files—or whatever it was this week—had gotten off to? How did you prove you didn't know a thing?

A fact about Max penetrated her unhappy thoughts. "Are you here on vacation?" she asked. "I noticed the Pennsylvania plates on your car."

"I'm on leave," he said tersely. Char understood the tone, which plainly indicated that he was not interested in discussing the matter further. She'd used the same tone herself when people asked why she was moving to northern Minnesota. "Trying to get some writing done," she'd said, which was true. Just not the whole truth. She wondered why Max was on leave. Had he been hurt? Was the department investigating a shooting he'd been involved in? Or was Internal Affairs looking into allegations of misconduct? She wished she knew. It would make a difference. Not that she'd ever trust a cop. Not after what she'd been through because of Theodore. She completely understood, on a rational level, why the authorities thought she had to know what he was involved in. But on an emotional level, it hurt. It hurt that people could think that of her when she'd always tried very hard—probably too hard, sometimes—never to harm anyone else.

A tense silence lengthened between them. She supposed he was waiting for her to ask the dreaded *why* question, which she had no intention of doing. At the same time, she couldn't think of anything else to say or ask. Or do.

Fortunately, she heard the sound of a heavy truck grinding in low gear down the road outside.

"I hear the Dumpster people now," she said in relief. Here was something to do, to distract them from whatever that lengthy silence had really been about.

Max glanced at his watch, a plain and serviceable model, and she remembered Theodore's flashy Rolex. She'd never understood the point of the Rolex. She thought Max would probably understand the point but think it was a ridiculous one to make.

"They're late," he muttered, which made her glad that she and Abby had been particularly punctual this morning.

Carefully stepping around the obstacles that impeded him, Max made his way out of the room. Char followed him, not having been given any instructions on what she should do otherwise.

They passed Abby in the hallway, where she sat cross-legged on the floor, leafing through old *Life* magazines. She hadn't been given her instructions either. Char left Abby to her reading and headed out to the front of the cabin with Max, who was directing the placement of the Dumpster as close to the front door as possible, while the two men who'd brought it debated the feasibility of that approach. Wisely, Char stayed out of their conversation and merely watched the ensuing spectacle with some amusement.

Cold Hands, Warm Hearts

If she hadn't seen the inside of the house, she would have wondered at the size of the Dumpster. Now she realized it was going to have to be dumped a couple of times before the place could be completely cleared.

"That's it," Max said, finally having accepted that he wasn't going to get exactly what he wanted, at least in re: Dumpster placement. He waved the truck driver and his helper off, and they finished doing whatever mysterious things they had to do before jumping into the truck and driving away.

When they were gone, Char and Max stood staring at the huge Dumpster, which seemed even larger now that the truck that had hauled it here was gone. Filling it up with the leftovers of an old lady's life was going to take a long time. As if in commentary, the sky started spitting snow.

"I feel exhausted already," Char said, crossing her arms as the wind sliced, freezing cold, across her. "How on earth did it get this way?" she asked. Then she wished she hadn't put it quite like that; it sounded highly critical of Max and his brother, and if there was one thing she knew by now, it was that you couldn't control what other people did, even your mother or your husband. Ex-husband. You could hope to influence them a little bit, but that was all.

"You didn't know my mother," Max said. "Although her apartment in town wasn't nearly this bad. And she wasn't always this way. I mean, she was always a saver." He grinned, a sudden memory, pleasant, must have crossed his mind. "She was always saying, 'Don't throw that out! It's a perfectly good whatsit.'"

"My mom was like that too. So of course I'm a real purger. I throw away even stuff I need. Which means Abby—"

"Is going to end up a pack rat like your mom." He smiled again, which she wished he wouldn't do, because it was a very nice smile, and she might want to see it again and try to think of ways to make him smile, which was ridiculous for a grown woman and potentially dangerous if it made her forget he was a cop.

"Anyway." Max turned to go back inside. She followed him and shut the door behind them. "Philip and I got busy with our own lives, and before we knew it—" He shrugged and gestured.

"This," she finished for him. "So where do we start?"

"You," Max pronounced carefully, "can start anywhere you want."

Char rolled her eyes, not caring if he saw her do it. "I meant Abby and me, not you and me." What did he think, she had fantasies of sorting through the trash with him?

"Just do what you can. Use your best judgment."

She gave him The Look, and he shrugged again. "If I'm around, I'll do my best to suggest a course of action. Otherwise, call Philip if you have any questions or problems."

Well, at least he wasn't a micromanager type. So far he wasn't really helpful either, but then, even he probably didn't have any idea where to start. She and Abby would just have to dig in and do the best they could.

"Do you care how much time I spend on this?" she asked. "I don't have a lot going on right now. But if you're trying to budget a certain number of hours per week . . ."

Max stared down at her for a long moment. She could feel his gaze, but she didn't look up; for some reason she didn't want to meet that flat gray gaze. Well, she knew the reason. He was unsettling. Her life was unsettling enough without taking him on.

Cold Hands, Warm Hearts

"Knock yourself out," he finally said, but Char had the sense that, despite his casual words, he was sympathetic. "We're not in any huge hurry," he went on. "Obviously, given that the place has been sitting here like this for the last couple of years. And we're not going to be able to find a buyer until spring."

Char nibbled on her lip, unsure how to bring up the next question. She didn't know Max or his brother's financial situation, but she didn't think a small-time veterinarian and a cop on leave possessed loads of resources. Of course, they had a bit more than she did, but how hard was that? Even so, she didn't want to take advantage. Neither Dr. Wilson nor Max struck her as a man who made a habit of getting taken advantage of, but still.

She cleared her throat. "I was just thinking, if you're on a budget, we could figure out the best way to do this without going over it." This was the part she always hated with clients, but usually she managed it a little better, without stumbling over the words so much.

"Don't worry about it," Max said. "The money comes out of the estate, not out of Philip's pocket or mine, and it has to be done before we can list the place with a broker. So . . ." He shrugged. "Just let Philip know the total hours each week."

Char didn't point out that if the money was coming out of the estate, it meant less would go to him and Dr. Wilson, so the money *was* coming out of their pockets. He'd no doubt figured that out. She let the matter drop. "You're definitely going to sell it?"

"Yeah. Neither one of us wants it."

"Well, no one would want it in this state," Char said. "But look at it. How beautiful it is."

He gave an eloquent glance around the jam-packed room.

"I mean the bones of the place. Once it's cleared out. This setting is so quiet and peaceful. And look how close to the lake it is. The view is unbelievable." She listened to herself and stopped. What was she doing? Trying to convince him to come be her next-door neighbor?

Max tamped the snow from his boots and said, "Philip built a small cabin on a lake a lot closer to his house, and I live in Philadelphia."

Char nodded. She supposed it wouldn't make much sense for the two of them to keep it under the circumstances. Still, wasn't it kind of sad to see things like this pass out of the family?

No, she told herself firmly. It was fine. Good, even, because it gave some other people a chance to build memories of summers on a lake. Better than letting it sit empty and useless.

Max climbed up the stairs to do battle with the electrical outlets again. She hoped he didn't electrocute himself or burn the house down. She heard a murmur as Max passed Abby in the hall. She took another look around the dismal interior and tried to summon her fighting spirit. There was so much to tackle. Where should she begin?

The kitchen, she decided. The light was best there. Until Max could get the electricity going again, it was going to be hard to see into the dark corners of the living room.

"Hey, Abby," she called up the stairs. "Time to get to work. See if Max has a spare battery lantern up there."

A minute later, Abby clambered down the stairs, lantern in hand. Char switched it on, then groaned at the disaster it revealed and was tempted to shut it off again.

Cold Hands, Warm Hearts

"There's sure enough to keep us busy for a while," she said, forcing a cheerful tone. She started by bringing armloads of newspapers and magazines to the Dumpster. Abby helped with the hauling, enjoying the act of flinging the paper into the Dumpster. Char had to rig a step so that she and Abby could reach over the side of the huge metal container, and at first she worried about Abby's tripping or slipping, especially as more snow accumulated, but Abby did fine, and she made herself stop worrying about it. Abby would be fine. They both would.

Once she'd cleared a path from the kitchen to the front door so they could move around more easily, she unearthed one end of the kitchen table and decided to use that as a work space. She had Abby continue to dump paper while she began to investigate the boxes stacked all around. The very first one she opened held dishes. Pulling away the newspaper covering, she saw a cup of fine bone china.

Char rocked back on her heels and wished she had a chair to sit in. She felt as if the wind had been knocked out of her. But she'd made the classic mistake of people who weren't pack rats: just because many of the accumulated objects were trash didn't mean they all were. "I can't throw this out," she said. She dug deeper and unwrapped another piece, this one a salad plate. Abby, arms full of newspapers, peered into the box, curious about what had grabbed her mom's attention.

"Plates," she said, her tone expressing how boring that was.

Char didn't try to set her straight. No eight-year-old could possibly appreciate what she'd just found. Rolling her sleeves up, she unwrapped all the contents of the box, just to see exactly what she'd found. She carefully stacked the dishes on the end of the kitchen table she'd cleared earlier.

Underneath a little dust, there were eight complete place settings of fine bone china without a chip or a crack on a single item. Of course, with her luck she'd change that the moment she started rewrapping everything. Still, she didn't have any intention of putting everything back into tattered old newspapers in a ratty old liquor-store box. A treasure like this needed bubble wrap and cushioning and special corrugated cardboard containers.

She set the empty box aside and stood, hands on hips, looking down at the result of her handiwork.

"I'll have to ask Max what he wants to do with this," she said, and she realized she'd need to start keeping track of things. A list of items needed—the aforementioned bubble wrap, for example—as well as an inventory of the valuable stuff. Assuming this box of china wasn't the only valuable item in the entire house.

Moth-eaten clothes filled the next two boxes, which made her doubt the likelihood that she'd discover anything else worthwhile, but finding trash certainly made her job easier. All she had to do was toss the boxes into the Dumpster. She did so, dusting her hands together with satisfaction as she headed back into the house. She passed Abby, who was getting rid of another armful of old newspapers, and wondered how quickly her daughter's enthusiasm for tossing things into the trash would wane.

Back in the kitchen, she couldn't see any difference all of her and Abby's work that morning had made, except that there was a pile of dishes on the table that hadn't been there before, which hardly seemed to show that they were going

Cold Hands, Warm Hearts

in the right direction. Even so, she could hardly let herself get discouraged so early in the process.

She turned to the stack of boxes nearest her, saying hello to her daughter when Abby came back into the kitchen. Opening another box yielded a collection of plates in a riot of colors.

"Vintage Fiesta ware," she breathed, an acquisitive urge she hadn't realized she possessed rearing its head and suggesting how pretty these would look in her own cupboards.

"More plates," said Abby, looking into the box.

"This stuff is so hot right now," Char said. She wasn't the only one with an acquisitive instinct, but other people had the bank accounts to back their urges up. "Okay, I have to talk to Max and Philip before I do anything with this. They can't have a clue what some of this stuff is worth."

She set the box of dishes aside. A creak of floorboards told her that Max was coming downstairs, so she went through the living room to meet him. His hair was standing up in agitated clumps, and he had a distracted expression on his face. Char repressed a smile and said with all the sympathy she could muster, "Not going well?"

Max started, his hand on the front door handle. He obviously hadn't seen her. He turned and said, "Well, when I came over this morning, I was asking myself, 'How hard can it be?'"

"And the answer is, harder than you thought?"

"They made it sound so simple at the hardware store."

"Of course," Char said. "How much equipment did they sell you?"

"They got their money's worth," he agreed. "I'm just going to get the electrician to do it."

"Good idea. Lights would help the process here. And what about the heater? I'm about to freeze to death."

"It's an oil heater, but it has an electric ignition, so once the electricity is on, it should work. I'm having someone come out to take a look at it before I do anything, though. And the phone service should be on in the next day or two."

"Which'll be great if you can find the phone. Or a jack to plug it into," Char said. "Have you got a second? I want you to look at something."

Max seemed reluctant to let go of the door, but he followed her into the kitchen, where she showed him the treasures she'd unearthed.

"This dishware is in amazing shape," Char said. "I can't throw it away. Not only would it be a crime against art, but this stuff is worth money."

Max did not seem impressed. He and Abby exchanged glances of complete understanding. "Plates," they said at the same time.

"Real money, Max."

"I don't have time to worry about it," he said. "And Philip—"

"I have an idea," Char interrupted. The idea had come to her full-fledged, which gave her hope that her creative instinct had not been completely extinguished by recent events but merely somewhat submerged. "I'll start an inventory and organize the things I think might be worth something. Once the trash is cleared, I'll arrange for some local antiques and collectibles dealers to make bids. Then, anything that they don't want, I could put on eBay and sell that way. I could arrange all of that for a commission on the sale price." She spoke in a rush, feeling a little like a

Cold Hands, Warm Hearts

used-car salesperson, even though it was an excellent idea no reasonable person would refuse.

Max didn't immediately answer. He went to the box of Fiesta ware and took out one of the plates. "I remember these," he said, rubbing his palm across the surface. "They come in different colors. Mom used them every day. They're worth something?"

"Yes," Char said. "I'd have to do some research but you can't put them in the trash. I mean, a bowl—one bowl—might sell for fifty dollars."

He put the plate back into the box. "It seems it would be easier to just donate the good stuff."

"Donate the proceeds," she suggested, "if you don't need the money yourself. But this kind of stuff should find the right home."

"The right home?" Max repeated. There was that eyebrow again. If she didn't think he was so darned attractive, she'd be able to see that quirking eyebrows and uninterested shrugs were not charming mannerisms but annoying characteristics.

"Yes," she said firmly. "The right home. Someone who appreciates them, knows what they are, values them."

"We wouldn't want them to go to the wrong home," he said, and though she knew he was teasing her, she said, "Exactly," and fixed him with a challenging look, daring him to laugh at her. He didn't.

"So you'd make sure everything found its rightful place, for a split of the proceeds."

"A commission on the sales price. Yes. That would be before expenses are deducted."

"Of course," he said gravely. "Well, I think I could twist Philip's arm and get him to agree to fifteen percent."

"Twenty," she said without missing a beat. Abby was turning out to be an excellent influence.

"You're on," Max said so promptly, she knew she could have asked for a lot more. *Drat.* Then she gave a mental shrug. Twenty percent had a nice ring to it, and it'd be easy enough to calculate. "Just be sure to keep track of everything. Philip will need good records to settle the estate."

"Of course," she said.

"Have at it." Then he said, "I should get going. I have some calls to make. I'll be back in a bit."

"All right. If it doesn't take long, come on over to my cabin when you're done. Abby and I will head over there in a bit to start lunch."

Max opened his mouth, and she had the impression that he meant to refuse her. Then he must have reconsidered, because he said, "That'd be great."

And yet for some reason, she didn't think he really meant it.

Once he was able to get a cell signal on the road a few miles from his mother's house, Max called the local electrician Philip had recommended, got a firm promise that he'd try to stop by sometime later in the day, took that for what it was worth, then in quick succession called the phone company, his brother—who agreed, a little distractedly, to Char's plan—then his boss to report in.

He almost hoped Abe wouldn't be in so he could just leave a message, but as luck would have it, Abe answered on the third ring.

"Max? What have you got for me? Have you made contact with the subject of the surveillance?"

Max rolled his eyes. (Abe couldn't see him do it, so no

harm, no foul). *Subject of the surveillance. Gotta love cop-speak.* "Yes. Char Simmons is living in the cabin next door to my mother's, and I've hired her to do some work there."

A charged silence. "I didn't authorize the disbursement of funds."

Oops. "Don't worry about it," Max said. "That part is completely legit. Philip, my brother—you remember, I told you he lives out here?—he's the one bankrolling the job."

"As long as you're not planning to submit an invoice. You know what the budget is like around here."

"No invoice, Abe."

"Okay. Have you established a viable cover?"

Max rolled his eyes again. *Yes, a perfectly viable cover.* "I'm playing a federal agent on leave, Abe."

Another charged silence. "You told her who you are?"

"She pretty much guessed."

"You used to be good at undercover work, Max," Abe said.

"Yeah, well, apparently it wore off."

"Do you feel in danger?"

"From *Char*?" What was she going to do, sic the Pomeranian on him? "No, Abe. I've got it under control."

"Good. Good. You know, the thing about developing a cover is that it gives you a certain amount of distance from the subject, which is sometimes necessary, you know. Whether she's a threat to you or not, it would have been better to establish yourself as a tradesperson or something."

Max though of his encounter with the wall outlets. "I think she might have been alerted to the fact that I'm not an electrician pretty early on."

"I'm just making the point because I don't want you thinking you can wade in and save the day for her."

"You're saying it's harder for a person to establish a real relationship with a subject if he lies about who he is."

"Exactly."

"And that's a good thing?"

"For an undercover agent, yes."

"I'm not undercover here, Abe. This is where I grew up."

A pause. "What does that mean, Max? I thought I understood that you'd agreed to keep an eye on her."

"I did. I will. If you're asking will I sell her down the river if and when the time comes, the answer is yes."

"But?"

"But I'm not going to lie to her about it."

A silence stretched out long enough that Max had to check his phone to make sure the call hadn't been dropped.

"You will do what you have to do?" Abe finally asked. "I'll take you off if I think you're too involved."

Which meant he'd set it up so that someone else got close to Char, and that person would lie to her, and the last thing Char and Abby needed right now were more lies.

"We don't have a problem, sir," he said, and Abe was apparently satisfied, because he didn't argue.

When Max hung up, he didn't like himself very well. He thought of Char with her dancing dark eyes, determined not to let circumstances get her down, and her fragile daughter, trying to behave as if everything was fine and had never been better.

He really hoped Char didn't know the first thing about anything her ex-husband might currently be up to. If she

Cold Hands, Warm Hearts 79

was abetting him, Max would do what he had to do. But he didn't want to.

Lunch was grilled cheese sandwiches with Abby's favorite side dish: Tater Tots. Max manfully ate the meal, thanked them both for their efforts, and then they all went back to the Wilson house, where he disappeared upstairs while Char and Abby returned to the kitchen.

They hadn't been at work long when Char heard a truck on the road outside. "Electrician's here!" she called up to Max.

"Finally," he said. "Send him up."

It had been a long time since she'd felt the companionship of just doing stuff with another adult, and it felt better than it should.

She opened the front door to the electrician, let him gawk at the cluttered interior for a moment, then sent him upstairs to Max. Earlier, she'd dug out her camera, and now she started taking photos of the plates, describing them in a notebook, and labeling the boxes. She wanted to be able to locate anything she needed later without having to look through every single box.

An hour, then two, passed quickly. Absorbed in her work, she didn't realize right away that Abby's chattering had ended some time previously. When she did, she went in search of her daughter, finding her sitting on the floor in an upstairs room, quizzing the men on what they were doing and why.

Being near Max, Char thought with a pang, and she hoped her daughter had better sense than to think of Max as a friend. She knew how much Abby missed having her daddy in her life; she'd soaked up Theodore's careless affection eagerly, and Max, though he was by no means careless, always made an effort to talk to her, neither condescending to her nor acting like she was a small adult.

Her heart went out for Abby. She wished there were something, anything, she could do about Theodore.

But there wasn't.

"Hey, sweetie," Char said, touching Abby's shoulder. "We're all done for now. Let's head back to our place for a nap."

"I don't need a nap."

Char didn't immediately address that remark. Instead she dug out a couple of dollars and paid Abby for her time. Abby put the money into a wooden chest she'd found in one of the upstairs bedrooms. Char accounted for the chest in the notebook, valuing it at a generous ten dollars. She'd deduct that from her first commission.

"We're heading home," she called out to Max. "See ya tomorrow."

In response she was rewarded with a grunt that said Max had heard but was involved in a complicated, manly task with the electrician and couldn't take the time to indulge in small talk.

Once back in their own cabin, Abby tucked her treasure chest in a dresser drawer in the bedroom.

"I'm going to buy some drawing paper," she announced. "And some pencils and stuff."

"Great idea," Char said. "Now, why don't you hop into bed and—"

"Why are you making me take a nap?" Abby demanded. Of course she seemed perfectly wide awake now. "I'm not a baby! I don't need a nap."

"I know you're not a baby," Char said. "But you need some rest. You almost fell asleep at the Wilson house."

"I'm not tired. I want to go back and do some more work."

"Sweetie, we're done for today."

"Whatever," Abby muttered, going into the bedroom alcove and shutting the door with more force than absolutely necessary.

Cinnamon looked up from her position on the daybed and barked.

"Not you too," Char said. She grabbed a coat and walked back outside. A quick walk around the property would help wake her up, and then she could get started on some of her own work—pitches to send, article ideas to flesh out, notes to editors. When she rounded the corner of the house, she saw that the lights were on in the Wilson house. Apparently Max and the electrician had succeeded in getting everything up and running without burning the house down. Yet, anyway. She hoped Max remembered to turn the heater on. It would be a lot easier to do her work there if she didn't have to wear a parka and gloves.

What was Max doing here? Getting the house ready to sell, yes, but she was pretty sure that wasn't the only reason he was here. The part of her that found him interesting and attractive hoped that he might be here because of her. The part of her that was used to suffering the effects of Theodore's poor choices worried that she was exactly the reason he was here, and it wasn't because he hoped he might be able to sneak a kiss before his leave ended and he went back to Philadelphia.

The bright pinks and oranges of the sunset, reflected in the water, caught her eye. The lake was starting to freeze over now, just as Keith had said it would. Hard to imagine all that water turning into a huge sheet of ice.

She walked to the shore and picked up a stone. She threw it into the lake, beyond the thin later of ice that had built up near the shore. The action was deeply satisfying on a physical, visceral level. She picked up another stone and weighed it in her hand. She gave it a heave, then heard the faint splash as it hit the water. No wonder Abby enjoyed the process so much. She threw another stone as far as she could and tried to see where it sank beneath the water. Mindless and calming, and fewer calories than eating cookies.

Wiping her hands on her jeans, she watched as the sunset faded, then picked her way carefully back to the cabin. The light spilling from the windows emphasized the darkness and the loneliness of their location.

When she looked over, the Wilson house was dark, and Max was gone.

Chapter Five

Abby crouched next to Max and stuck her face close to the open toolbox by his knee.

"What's that?" she asked. Her hands were clasped behind her back because he had already warned her not to touch—to which admonition she'd rolled her eyes and said, "I know," as if she were already a teenager, giving him a moment's pity for Char. But at least she listened to him. Plenty of people didn't.

"What's what?" he asked, peering around the drawer that was stuck on its runner. Why was he trying to figure out why the drawer wasn't working properly? He was a cop, not a handyman.

"That," Abby said, gesturing with her chin. His fault for telling her not to touch; obviously she didn't even dare point. He sighed and said, "Describe it."

"That silver thing with the round thing on the end."

Well, that clarified matters.

"It's a socket wrench," he guessed, then immediately felt guilty. What if she meant the pipe wrench? She'd be calling it by the wrong name for the rest of her life, and he would have only himself to blame.

He bumped the drawer with the heel of his hand. When all else failed, the application of brute force sometimes produced the desired effect. Although not in this case.

"What's it for?"

He looked up from his labors. For all the dark circles under her eyes and the wicked scar on her partially shaved head, she was like every other kid he knew. The only difference was that she came equipped with Char, and he felt a dull sense of shame for interacting with her and making her believe he was her friend when for all he knew he'd be arresting her mother before the end of the year.

What kind of man could look at Abby, so delicate and fragile, and contemplate bringing her mother to justice? Because he was starting to worry that he was going to have to make a choice between what was just, legally speaking, and what was right, and the last time he'd faced a moral dilemma . . .

His partner had almost died.

He pushed the thought aside before all of the memories and regrets could start crowding in.

"Hey, Max," Abby said, "if you don't know, you can just say so."

Max recalled that she'd asked him a question. "I do know," he said. "I know what all of those tools are for, or I wouldn't have them in the toolbox in the first place."

"Excellent," Abby said. "Then what's that? And what do you do with it?" She spared a glance at him in his labors. "You know, Mom just uses soap."

"Soap?" The non sequitur left him a little confused.

"On the drawer. So it doesn't stick anymore."

"Oh." That made sense, and he supposed he'd known about that fix but hadn't remembered it.

Cold Hands, Warm Hearts 85

"Mom knows everything," Abby said helpfully. "Except I don't think she knows what that is." This time her hand came around, and she poked at one of the tools with her finger.

"To be honest," Max said, "I'm not sure what that is either."

"I'm starving," Char called up the stairs. "Either of you slackers want some lunch?"

Abby popped to her feet and ran to the door. "We're not slackers! We're working very hard."

"It's suspiciously quiet for people working hard," Char said.

"We fixed the dresser!" Abby countered.

"Then I'll eat my words," Char said. "But I'd rather eat lunch. Are you *coming*?"

Abby slanted a glance at Max. "She's very impatient."

"So I've noticed."

"Come on," Abby said, grabbing his hand. "She'll eat all the potato chips." She dragged him out of the room. He saw that Char had already set out for her cabin, naturally expecting him to follow with Abby.

It didn't help his guilty feelings to take advantage of Char's generosity while trying to find out of if she'd abetted a suspected felon. Every job had its unpleasant aspects, he reminded himself, and he went to set the table.

He was just filling the glasses— tap water for Char and him, milk for Abby—when Abby came back in from letting the dog out.

"Wash your hands," Char said without looking up from slicing the thick loaf of bread on the counter.

"Dogs are cleaner than humans."

"Wash your hands anyway."

"You don't make me wash my hands every time I hug you."

"I'm about to start," Char said, and Max could hardly blame her.

"So when can we call Daddy?"

Max almost dropped the pitcher of water but managed to set it on the table with a loud thump. Char had gone stiff. There could be more than one reason for that, but he watched her carefully. She moved to the stove to stir the stew that bubbled on the burner.

"Honey, we've talked about that," she said, giving Max a sidelong look. What did that mean? What had they discussed about Abby's father? And why was Char so reluctant to talk about it in front of him? He busied himself with folding napkins and putting them next to plates.

"But I want to talk to Daddy!"

"I'd like to have a word with him myself," Char said. She threw an apologetic glance in Max's direction. "Her dad's been busy and unavailable, which isn't like him, so of course it bothers Abby a lot." She gave a smile, and she must have known how unconvincing it was, because she let it go after a moment.

"Can you set the trivet out?" she asked Abby, whose mouth was set in a mutinous line. But she did as her mother asked. Char moved the stew pot to the table and said brightly, "Let's eat," and then Max found himself trying to break the tension when he knew for a fact that allowing tension to continue was the best way to get information. People often revealed more than they intended or blurted out explanations when they were uncomfortable.

"Any plans for Thanksgiving?" he asked and then, without planning, added, "You two could join us." Philip and Elaine would be surprised, but they wouldn't mind, and if Max wasn't mistaken, they'd both agree it was a good idea. He was so busy justifying himself to himself that he almost missed the expression of astonishment, followed by reluctance, that crossed Char's face.

"Can we?" Abby asked, *her* expression ecstatic. "It would be so much fun!"

When Char turned to him, her face was so pleased that he wondered if he'd imagined her earlier reaction. "We'd love to come," she said. "What time should we be there? And what can we bring?"

On Thanksgiving Day, they drove to Dr. Wilson's house together. Char had asked for directions, and Max had offered to pick them up, and she'd argued that it was ridiculous for him to drive all the way out from his brother's house just to get them and bring them back. But he'd insisted and won the argument. Char got the feeling that he would win most of the arguments he set his mind to winning. She wished, not for the first time, that she had found a way to weasel out of the invitation.

Max had been nothing but kind and helpful over the last few days, and he hadn't done any prying or given any sign that he was thinking like a cop instead of a man. She was responding to the man, but she was deeply worried about the cop.

They arrived at Dr. Wilson's place, an old, comfortable-looking farmhouse. Max opened the car door for Char and then for Abby, which made Abby giggle—Char really needed to have a talk with her daughter about being susceptible to masculine charm—and then Max led the way up the walk and opened the front door to yell, "We're here!"

Without waiting for an answer, he walked right in as if he owned the place. Maybe that was what a family did. Char had never really had that experience. When Abby was grown and living on her own, would she fling open the door to Char's house and call out, "I'm here!" as if she owned the place?

Char hoped so.

"Come in, come in," Char heard a woman say from inside. The voice didn't belong to Kate, so she assumed it was Kate's mother, whom Char hadn't met. Char hung back a little, wiping her feet on the mat and taking her time hanging up her coat and Abby's on the rack. While she was busy with that, Max took Abby's hand and brought her down the hall.

"Hey, everyone," Char heard Max say. "This is Abby, Elaine." He glanced over his shoulder. Char hurried to join him. She didn't want Dr. Wilson or his wife to feel insulted by her reluctance to come in. *They* weren't the reason she was nervous about this.

"And here's Char," Max said. His voice changed as he said her name, but Char didn't quite understand why or what it meant.

"Hi," Char said, stepping into the kitchen and putting a hand on Abby's shoulder as much for the reassuring physical contact as to claim her. Dr. Wilson and his wife and daughter were putting together the Thanksgiving meal in the warm, rambling kitchen, already filled with the delicious smell of roasting turkey. "Thanks for having us."

"Happy to have you," Dr. Wilson said, abandoning the celery he was stuffing and going to the sink to wash his

Cold Hands, Warm Hearts

hands. Char peeked over at the stove, where giblets for gravy simmered. Her stomach gave an anticipatory growl. "Let me show you around. Max, you and Abby might just see if Elaine will share that coffee cake she made this morning." He shot a glance at Char and said, "I'm assuming Abby would rather eat cake than take the grand tour?"

From the way he said it, Char had the impression that he wanted to talk to her alone, so she answered, "That'd be fine."

"I was just about to offer," Elaine said with a smile, crimping the edge of a pumpkin pie, then wiping her hands on a dish towel before reaching for plates in the cabinet.

Char glanced over her shoulder as she followed Dr. Wilson out of the kitchen. Abby was eagerly taking a seat next to Kate, and Elaine was leaning forward to ask her something, probably how big of a slice she wanted.

Dr. Wilson was so lucky to have a family like this. Did he know? How much she had wanted this for herself and had never been able to manage it. Sometimes she wondered if she'd tried too hard, and if that was part of the problem. Grabbing the wrong thing in an effort to get what she wanted, not realizing the difference right away.

"You have a nice family," she said.

"They are indeed," Dr. Wilson said.

"So tell me a little about the house," she said, since that was the ostensible reason for their tour. They'd come into a roomy living room from the eat-in kitchen, and she saw a number of intriguing doors leading off from the room.

"Traditional Minnesota farmhouse, built over a hundred years ago," said Dr. Wilson. "It's been in the family ever since the beginning. You can see where my parents knocked out walls to combine rooms." He pointed toward one door. "That leads upstairs to a couple of bedrooms tucked under the eaves. That one leads to a mudroom. And that one's a closet."

That seemed about it for the tour of the house. What did he want?

"Let's take a walk around the property," he suggested.

She agreed, though she didn't really want to get back into her coat and gloves.

"Lots of Minnesota families have Norwegian ancestry," Char said as she pulled those articles of clothing back on. "What about yourself?"

"Norwegian, Irish—a bit of everything," Dr. Wilson said.

That seemed to be that. He wrapped a scarf around his neck, then led the way outside.

When the door was firmly shut behind them, he said, "This house came from my mother's side of the family. Very practical people—have been from the start. We're farmers, mechanics, that kind of thing."

Char had the sense that they were getting to the important part. "You're a veterinarian," she remarked, not because it was an impractical career choice, but because he'd left it off the list. It wasn't a huge leap to go from farming to being a veterinarian, although it would have required a dedication to education and either a certain amount of wealth or a crushing student-loan debt. Or maybe—she was nothing if not cynical—he'd married money.

"A vet is just a glorified mechanic," Dr. Wilson said. "How's that Pom of yours?"

"She's good as new."

"Thought she would be."

Cold Hands, Warm Hearts 91

That seemed to exhaust that line of discussion.

Dr. Wilson gestured at a patch of tilled ground. "Here's the kitchen garden Elaine keeps. She's a therapist for a mental-health clinic. All of her hobbies are productive."

"Practical," Char said, catching his drift. Fine, they were practical people. Was the whole point of this conversation to point out that she wasn't practical and he could give her pointers?

"She'll have winter squash coming along until the worst of winter. You should see her root cellar."

"I didn't know people had those anymore."

"We do. Practical people, you see. Except Max."

"Max?" Char echoed, incredulous. "Max? He strikes me as the most practical one of the lot." She thought of his taking care of his mother's house. The way he got results when he determined he needed other people's assistance. Even the way he held himself.

"That's what he thinks too," Dr. Wilson said. "Thinks I'm the dreamer, trying to make a go of a lifestyle that passed out of fashion seventy years ago. But look at him. What about his job? That wasn't prompted by his desire to wrestle with the tough and gritty problems of ordinary people but by idealism, pure and simple."

The way he said *idealism* made it sound like a bad word.

"I'm sure his job is tough and gritty," Char said, then wondered why she felt the need to defend Max.

"Me too," said Dr. Wilson. "This way," he added, leading her down a rutted path that led away from the house and garden. In the suburbs, the path would have been paved with stone tiles, but here someone had thrown down gravel a long time ago—so long ago that most of it was missing now. A dusting of snow made walking slightly hazardous, so she focused on where she was putting her feet as Dr. Wilson talked. Maybe if she fell and twisted her ankle, they wouldn't have to have this conversation. She was pretty sure she knew where it was headed.

"But he doesn't do the job because he wants to wrestle with tough and gritty problems," Dr. Wilson explained. "Unlike me. When I'm dealing with livestock, I have to keep in mind the animal's condition, its suffering, and the owner's goals and resources. Balancing all of them is what makes my work useful. If everyone had as much money as he needed to solve every problem he had with an animal, I wouldn't really be that much use."

"Uh-huh," Char said. She supposed *practical* was one way of looking at what he'd done for her: healed her dog without worrying how she would afford it, discounting the price he charged her, then finding her a job to be able to pay him back. So, yeah, practical. Also kindhearted, generous, and compassionate.

Dr. Wilson didn't look at her as he continued talking. "That's why what happened has shaken him so. It altered his sense of self. He's always thought of himself as a practical and straightforward man. He doesn't think of himself that way anymore."

"What happened?"

He turned to her, rubbing his red nose and peering through his glasses at her. "If he hasn't told you the story, it's not my place to do so."

If *that* wasn't annoying . . . Why had he brought her out here, if not to gossip about Max? "He was shot, wasn't he?" Char guessed. "While he was working a case."

Dr. Wilson shook his head, clucking his tongue. "Now, don't go doing that. I expect better of you, Char."

Char stumbled a little on the path. What was she doing, and why did Dr. Wilson expect better of her? "Me? What am I doing?"

"He's a romantic at heart," Dr. Wilson said, and he sniffed. "And I don't want you succumbing to that." She could practically hear the *Are you listening, young lady?* that he didn't say. "It's not the noble, self-sacrificing situation you've probably imagined."

Char hadn't imagined any situation at all, because this was the first she'd learned anything about the actual reason Max was on leave. She said indignantly, "I don't know what you're talking about. I haven't imagined anything. But if it isn't that way, then what way is it?"

"Not my place," Dr. Wilson repeated.

Was there anything more aggravating than a man who made cryptic comments and then refused to expand on them out of some misguided sense that the person he was talking about deserved some privacy?

"Here we go," he said a minute later, stopping at a fence. He rested his arms against it. "Here's where I graze the horses. They're actually in the stable right now." He pointed to a gray, weather-beaten wooden building that looked like a very long garage. "We've got three horses, one for each of us. We like to ride together when we get the chance. Plus the pony, of course."

"Of course."

He nudged her with his elbow and pointed to another weather-beaten wooden building, this one smaller than the stables and surrounded by a chain-link fence. "Over there is the goat pen."

"They have goats at a petting zoo back home," Char said. "Abby loves them."

"Little girls always do. Romantics at heart."

"What do you mean?" She wasn't sure how liking to pet goats made a person romantic at heart.

"Goats are ornery and only care about eating," Dr. Wilson clarified. "Little girls think they can change them if only they love them enough."

Char grinned. "That sounds about right." Abby always took the petting zoo goats' interest in the corn she fed them as evidence of the affection they had for her. Still, she had to smile at Dr. Wilson, the old fraud. "Practical, right. Look around. How is this practical? How can you possibly call this spread, this lifestyle, practical? You're a romantic at heart too."

Dr. Wilson shook his head firmly. "I'm not the romantic one. Who sees the damsel in distress and goes haring off to rescue her?"

"I don't know. Who?" Char asked, though he was obviously referring to Max. She was no damsel and didn't need any rescuing, and she was pretty sure she resented the implication that she did. "You took care of Cinnamon," she pointed out, trying not to blush at the thought of Max—not to mention Dr. Wilson—thinking she needed rescuing. "You fixed her and gave me a job and reduced your usual rates."

"See?" Dr. Wilson said, stabbing a forefinger at her. "Exactly my point. Practical. Hurt animal? Fix it. Woman out of money? Find her a job." He was totally serious. She could tell by the expression on his face.

"Whereas Max . . . ?"

"Whereas Max suddenly decided to spend all of his spare time at Silver Lake to keep a benevolent eye on you, though from what I can make out, he's more of a burden on you than an aid. You're fixing his meals and doing most of the hard work in getting the house cleaned up. See? You're like me. Practical."

Char blinked, not sure how to respond. No one had ever accused her of being practical before. She was going to have to think about how she felt about that.

"Over here is the barn," Dr. Wilson said, moving away from the fence. Char looked obediently at the barn. It looked like everything a barn should be, second-story hayloft and all, except it wasn't painted red. "We don't run cattle anymore. Too much work and not enough money in it."

Char was pretty sure the profit motive wasn't the main reason Dr. Wilson did anything, but she kept her mouth shut.

"Just beyond is another pasture and pond." He made a dismissive gesture with one hand.

"Do you grow any crops?" Char asked, following him down a muddy path. Apparently he intended to give her a closer look at the barn, even though she was of the opinion that if you'd seen one barn, you'd seen them all.

"Some alfalfa hay. The neighbor mows it"—another wave of the hand, apparently indicating the direction of the neighbor's residence—"and we split it. And Elaine has the vegetable garden you saw. Although you can't really call that cropland. I don't have time to tend to crops." He sounded a little quarrelsome, even though she hadn't expressed an opinion about the lack of crop growing.

"I can imagine," she said.

"Right. You're practical." He paused and said, "All I intended to say was that he hasn't had an easy time of it."

They were back to Max. "Okay," Char said cautiously.

Did Dr. Wilson think she was some sort of femme fatale, collecting men's hearts and stomping on them? If so, she was a little flattered. No one had ever mistaken her for a femme fatale before. "I'll be gentle," she promised.

Dr. Wilson turned away from the door and fixed her with a look. "You think I'm overreacting, don't you?"

"I just have a hard time imagining Max as the vulnerable type. He seems as if he can take care of himself."

"Oh, he *seems*," Dr. Wilson scoffed. "He's my brother. He's a romantic idiot, but I don't want to see him get hurt."

Dr. Wilson seemed a little fixated on the subject of the practical versus the romantic nature, though he must know everyone possessed some quantity of both.

"I'm not going to hurt him," Char said. She tried to set his mind at ease. "We're just friends." Whatever Dr. Wilson thought, she and Max were in no danger of developing the kind of relationship where someone might get hurt. Least of all Max. If anyone was going to get hurt, it was Char, for hanging out with a cop.

"Friends." Dr. Wilson's tone said he'd heard that line before. He rolled his eyes in case she hadn't noticed his opinion. "Well, don't let him get confused."

"He doesn't seem that easy to confuse," Char said.

"He's a romantic idiot," Dr. Wilson reiterated. "Damsel in distress, he must be the knight in shining armor, you see?"

What Char saw was that *Dr. Wilson* was the romantic idiot, though she would never have offended him by saying so. "I don't need a knight," she said.

"Sure," said Dr. Wilson. "*I* know that, and *you* know that, but does *he* know that?"

* * *

Char felt a little self-conscious as she made her way back to the kitchen where Abby was helping Elaine scrub potatoes. She'd never had such a weird conversation about her love life, and she wasn't sure how she felt about it, though she knew Dr. Wilson had only broached the subject out of the best of intentions.

"We're making mashed potatoes!" Abby exclaimed, brandishing the scrubber. "With real potatoes!"

"Ah, busted," Char said. "Abby is accustomed to seeing mashed potatoes come out of a box."

"That's how Mom usually makes them," Kate said from the depths of the pantry, where she appeared to be unearthing platters and serving utensils. "But it's Thanksgiving, and on Thanksgiving we do everything the hard way."

Char slanted a glance in Max's direction. He had a cup of coffee and the newspaper in front of him, and he didn't look anything like a knight in shining armor. He hadn't even shaved.

"Anything I can do to help?" she asked.

"These potatoes need to be peeled," Elaine said. "Abby and Kate are going to set the dining room table."

"We are?" Kate asked.

"And Max is going to help with the potatoes," Elaine announced.

"Sure thing," Max said, giving Kate a pointed look and setting the newspaper aside.

"You would be a more convincing role model if you *offered* to do the work that needs to be done," Kate pointed out, dumping an armload of dishes onto the table next to him. "Instead of waiting for Mom to tell you."

"The day I'm a role model is the day your parents are

going to be very afraid," Max said lightly. He went to the sink, took the potato Elaine was holding out of her hands, bumped her out of the way, steered Abby in Kate's direction, then opened a drawer and pulled out two paring knives. Presenting one to Char with a flourish, he said, "I do know my way around a kitchen."

"Then you can be in charge of lunch from now on."

"Ah, you mistake me for someone who has something to prove."

"But you do have something to prove," Char said. "Show me your stuff. Whoever peels the most potatoes in the next half hour is relieved of kitchen duty until Christmas."

"Only if Elaine judges the quality of the handiwork."

"You're on," Char said, and then he smiled, and she knew that even if she won the contest, she'd just lost the war.

Chapter Six

Char slept hard and only awoke when she felt the weight of an eight-year-old on her back. Abby leaned forward, pulled Char's hair away from her face, and said into her ear, "Whatcha doing?"

"What do you think?" Char groaned. "I'm sleeping."

"Get out of bed, you sleepyhead," Abby chanted, climbing off her back and rolling over to snuggle against Char's side. For a moment Char thought Abby might be content with that, but then she announced, "We have to work today, Mom! You'd better get up."

"Hey! Who's the boss?" Char gave a fake growl, and Abby giggled and got to her feet.

Half an hour later, cleaned, fed, and dressed, they made their way across the yard to the Wilson place. Char saw a handyman's van and Max's car in the driveway. She hesitated at the door. Yesterday's camaraderie had been very appealing, but she would be an idiot if she thought it meant anything. And yet, standing out here in the cold, telling herself not to have any expectations, meant that she was having expectations.

She sighed and pushed open the front door. She heard

Max moving around upstairs as she went into the house. "Hey, we're here," she called out, and she squelched the desire to go upstairs and say hello to him, face-to-face, as if she couldn't wait to see him. By golly, she could wait. She could wait even if it killed her.

She and Abby went to work, the day off having given them both renewed energy. With one ear, she listened for the sound of the floorboards creaking in the way that meant Max was headed for the stairs. When she heard the sound, she grabbed an armload of trash and headed outside with it. Abby gave her a suspicious look—trash-dumping was Abby's job, after all, not Char's—but fortunately didn't say anything.

Char timed the task so that when she came back into the house, she met Max in the hallway. He was talking with an older man, presumably the heater-repair person the van in the driveway promised.

"Thanks," Max was saying. He shook the man's hand, and a flurry of receipts and checks changed ownership. Then the older man tipped his cap at Char and left the house.

"Don't put that away just yet," Char said, when Max went to tuck the checkbook back into his pocket. She reached into her own pocket and produced an envelope, which she handed to him. "That's the invoice for last week. Dr. Wilson said you were handling the details."

"I am," Max said. He took the invoice, glanced at it, then at her. "Whatever happened to thirty days net?"

"I'm a due-on-delivery kind of woman," Char said. "Like the heater repairman."

"Ah." He wrote out a check and handed it to her, and she folded it and put it into her pocket.

Max shoved her invoice and his checkbook into his back pocket. They would probably fall out as he worked today, and he'd wonder what had happened to them, but that was not her problem.

"Heater all fixed?" she asked.

"Yep. Can't you feel it?"

"Ah. I knew there was something different about this place today. I'm not freezing to death."

"Yeah." He shifted and seemed to have something more to say, but then he didn't say it. He turned to head up the stairs.

"I told Dr. Wilson I'm finding some valuable collectibles," she said brightly. Why? Was she trying to prolong her contact with Max? Because, if so, she was nuts.

"I'm pretty sure he'd be glad to have you call him Philip. Everyone else does."

But he seemed like a Dr. Wilson, not a Philip. Char didn't argue the point, though. "Anyway, I'm cataloguing everything the way I said. I'll arrange for local dealers to take a look later, when we're closer to being done here."

"That's good."

"Okay. I'm just updating you because Dr. Wilson—Philip—said you were in charge of all this."

"I'll be here," Max said.

"Oh, okay," Char said. What was that supposed to mean? He'd been here all along.

"I'm going to be staying here," he clarified after a moment had passed.

"Here?" Her voice squeaked a little. It was bad enough working with him in the same house during the day. But to have him as her next-door neighbor . . .

"I see," she said, although she didn't really. "Did

you—will we be in the way? Would you rather do the cleanup yourself?"

"God, no," Max said, looking appalled. "No. We can continue the way we've been doing everything. I just thought I'd mention it. Now that the electricity is working and the heater is running and the pump for the well water is going, it seems like as good a time as any to move in."

"Right," Char said. "Well. That's good. I mean, it'll make me and Abby feel less isolated." Knowledge dawned, and she felt her face turn red. *He thinks he's a knight in shining armor.* "You're not doing this because of us?" she demanded.

"No, of course not," he said hastily, but something in the way he said it made her not quite believe it. "It's just that Philip and I get a bit on each other's nerves, and since I'm going to be here a lot of the time anyway . . ." He shrugged, as if it made perfect sense, which, maybe, it did. Just because she thought it would be wonderful to have a family, getting on one another's nerves and all, didn't mean Max necessarily relished being in close quarters with his relatives. It was too bad, but she wasn't going to criticize.

How long was he planning to live here? It didn't sound as if he was talking about staying for just a few days. He made it sound, if not permanent, then at least long-term.

"I thought you were a cop in Philly," she said.

"I am."

"Isn't that a bit of a commute?"

Max gave a reluctant smile. "I told you, I'm on leave."

"Yes, you did. I was thinking it was temporary. For a few days."

Max's eyes slid away from hers. "Yeah, well. I'll be

here a little while longer." He didn't elaborate any further, and she didn't push. If he wanted to share, he would.

"Okay. So I'll just . . ." He gestured toward the stairs.

"Oh, sure," Char said. What did he do up there all day long? She supposed he was cleaning out one of the bedrooms, but she hadn't seen much progress. She didn't ask about that either.

"Lunch at twelve," she reminded him.

"It'll be soup and crackers," he warned her.

"That's fine," she said. He wasn't going to get out of losing the potato-peeling contest that easily. With a wave of a hand, she headed back into the kitchen.

Abby was there, sitting cross-legged on the floor, and was opening the flaps on one of the boxes. "Oh, wow," she said, sticking her hand into the interior.

"What's in there?"

"Dead things."

Char leaped forward, her heart hammering in her throat. Abby withdrew a moth-eaten fur stole and showed it to her. Char closed her eyes thankfully and sank to the floor next to Abby.

"Ugh," she said.

"Yeah," Abby agreed, wiping her fingers on her jeans and reaching for a different box.

After another few hours of steady work, Char got up, creaking to her feet. Abby had settled on a blanket she'd unearthed—Char tried not to think of what kinds of dirt and germs it might be harboring—and was leafing through old *National Geographic* magazines and regaling Char with outdated information about countries that no longer existed. There. Homeschooling accomplished for the day, Char thought, when she explained that Ceylon was now called Sri Lanka, and Yugoslavia had splintered into more countries than she could enumerate, though she tried. When Abby's interest flagged, right around the time Char's knowledge of Balkan states floundered, she said, "Time for lunch."

She got to her feet and went into the hallway. "Hey, Max!" she called up the stairs. "Lunch! Abby and I are starving."

Max peered out of the front bedroom. He was carrying a box. That was the result of all his effort? One box? Maybe she could give him some pointers.

"What?" he said, as if he was surprised at the time—or maybe that she'd actually expected him to fulfill his end of the bargain.

"Lunch. Remember? Soup and crackers?"

"Oh, sure." He glanced around, then said, "Let me just get rid of this."

Char gave him a skeptical glance. "You sure that's all trash?" Could he be trusted to tell trash from treasures? She wasn't certain.

"I'm very sure," he said. "Although I admit that someone might find electric bills from ten years ago and old *Reader's Digest* condensed books a treasure trove, I somehow doubt it."

"Oh. You're right. Trash."

Abby headed into the bedroom for a nap, taking Cinnamon with her. Cinnamon, not ready for a rest, had been shanghaied anyway and pacified with a handful of treats that Abby knew she wasn't supposed to take into the bedroom but that Char was too tired to forbid her to do.

"Thanks for lunch," she said.

Max had been mostly quiet throughout the meal, leaving the chattering to Abby, who kept it up until she yawned abruptly and her eyelids lowered as if a switch had been turned off.

"I'll do the dishes," Char said, although she didn't move from her spot at the table. She rested her cheek on one fist and considered taking a nap too. But she couldn't do that with Max sitting there, and he seemed in no great hurry to head back to the Wilson house.

He leaned back in his chair and said, "So how'd you end up here? This is the wrong season to spend in a fishing cabin on a lake."

Char's shoulders tightened, but she forced herself not to take the comment as a criticism. She told him, lightly, the same story she told everyone she didn't know very well, about inheriting the cabin and wanting a quiet place to do some writing.

He nodded once. "But doesn't it seem a little risky? With Abby the way she is? Just to get some writing done?"

Char felt her smile go brittle. She wished people wouldn't jump to conclusions so easily and make snap judgments so quickly. But then, she reminded herself, if she didn't tell all of the facts, what did she expect? She looked at Max and debated confiding in him. But that seemed as if it could have a worse outcome than letting him make a judgment about her.

"Not that it's any of my business," he added, when she didn't answer.

"No," she said. "It's not any of your business." It was irritating to think he'd assume that she'd take a risk without a good reason, but at the same time, he didn't know her very well, and maybe she seemed like the kind of person who would. But she couldn't help saying, "Just like why you're on leave isn't any of my business." She got to her feet and started clearing dishes.

"You're right," he said. He rose to help her carry dishes, but she snapped, "I can get it, thanks anyway."

"Okay." He held up his hands in surrender, but she noticed he didn't go anywhere. Instead, he walked to the bank of windows that faced out over the lake and stood looking out. She turned her back on him and filled the dishpan with hot, sudsy water. The cleanup took only a minute. Without Abby to wield the dishtowel, she left the dishes in the rack to dry, then neatened up the kitchen. By the time she was done, she'd recovered her temper, and she was glad Max hadn't left and sought refuge away from her at the Wilson house.

Though he didn't turn around at her entrance, he must have heard her come into the living room, because he gestured at the window and said, "Look at that."

Char came to stand next to him, fascinated by what she saw. The day had darkened while they were eating, which she had noticed and Abby had commented on. Now the snow had come, suddenly and all-encompassing. It came in sheets, like a downpour, but it wasn't rain, and it was quiet, unaccompanied by a howling wind. It was eerie and fascinating, unlike anything she'd seen before. She took an unthinking step a little closer to Max.

"That is so bizarre," she said. "I didn't even know it was coming."

"That's how travelers get into trouble up here," he said.

"I wouldn't want to be out in it, that's for sure. I've seen a lot of snow in my life, but I have never been in a snowstorm where you literally couldn't see anything, just a sheet of white."

"Hope it doesn't go on for three days like it's been known to do."

"Three days?" Char demanded. "You're joking."

"Not at all." Then he added, "And let's hope the furnace doesn't go out."

She turned to give him a look. "Try not to be so optimistic, Max. Give it to me straight. I can take it."

A smile tugged his lips, and he said, "I'm sure you educated yourself before you decided to spend the winter up here."

"I did," Char said, turning back to the window. At least he had a better opinion of her common sense than she'd thought. "But just reading and hearing about something is different from actually experiencing it." She slanted him a sidelong look. "And I do have wood." Then, because she wanted to prove something, even though she despised the impulse—she didn't have anything to prove to anyone, not even Max—she added, "I split it myself."

"Better you than me," Max said. "I got out of this part of the country for a reason."

"Tired of chopping wood?"

Max shrugged. "It's different up here," was all he said.

"Closer to the bone?"

"Closer to the bone," he agreed. He turned away from the window. "Hope you don't mind, but I'm not going out in that even though my place isn't far."

"It'd be easy to get lost and wind up in the lake," she said. Then she added, "Sure, stay. Make yourself at home. I wasn't planning to do any more work until after Abby's nap anyway."

He unearthed a deck of cards from the cabinet by the front door. How had he known where they were? She narrowed her eyes at him, suspicions that she'd previously stilled ruffling again. Had he been in the cabin when she wasn't here, looking around? Maybe at a time when she thought he was upstairs at the Wilson house, wrestling with outlets? He was a cop, and cops were curious.

But surely he'd respect her privacy. Wouldn't he?

"I know sixty-seven ways to play cards," Max said meditatively, and then, as if that sparked a memory he didn't want to think about, he tossed the deck of cards onto the table and walked across the living room.

"If you're a pacer, I withdraw my offer for you to stay until the storm clears up," Char said. "It gives me ulcers to watch people pace."

"I'm not a pacer," Max said, going to the window.

"Oh. You're a watcher. That's almost worse," Char said with a grin, collecting the cards he'd abandoned and shuffling them together.

"How does Abby's father feel about you being up here with Abby? To write?"

Char started, surprised he'd brought up the subject again. Obviously, it bothered him on some level. Why?

"Just wondering why he didn't offer to help out, if things were tough for you. I mean, if I had a kid, and her mom was having some financial troubles, I wouldn't be able to just stand by and watch."

Char concentrated on laying out a hand of solitaire. Oh, that was what he *said,* but was it true? In Max's case, she conceded it might be.

"He doesn't know," Char said, moving an ace of clubs and turning over a four of hearts. "I haven't been able to talk to him about it."

Max glanced over his shoulder, but though he seemed

casual and relaxed, she knew she'd been right to call him a watcher. That was what he was doing now, watching. Not just with his eyes but with all of his senses, listening and seeing and sensing.

"Why not?"

They were beyond superficial small talk now. Only one of Char's closest friends—Deanna—knew the whole story. She had no good reason to tell it all to Max except that she wanted him to know. To get his good opinion? Why did that matter? Well, she knew why it did.

She examined the cards on the table without really seeing them and said, "As near as I can figure it, he liquidated everything he could and stopped making payments on anything he owed that he couldn't unload for ready cash. Like his car lease, utility bills, that kind of thing. He may have tried to sell his house but couldn't—it went into foreclosure. Then he embezzled all the funds from his law firm, including money from escrow accounts, and took off for parts unknown, leaving his partner holding the bag. He even stopping paying his health insurance premiums, which I didn't know until it was too late."

"Abby?" The question was terse and cut right to the heart of the matter.

"Yes."

"He left you and Abby high and dry? He didn't warn you?"

"First I knew was at the hospital when they discovered Abby's brain tumor."

"Unbelievable," Max said, although surely he'd seen people do much worse things in his time as a cop. It was all too believable to Char.

"I should have been more careful," she said, frowning at

the cards in front of her. "We had a divorce settlement that spelled it out, but I should have—"

"Why are you blaming yourself?" he asked reasonably. "You had an agreement and no reason to think he wouldn't keep it."

That was the sticking point, wasn't it? She'd known that Theodore was capable of lying and cheating. "If only I had—"

"If wishes were horses, beggars would ride," Max said, coming over to sit next to her. "As my mother used to say. That six can go onto the seven."

She moved the card in question. He seemed to have dropped the question of Theodore, which suited her just fine.

"What was your mother like?" Char asked, picking what she hoped was a safer topic of conversation—or at least one that made her less uncomfortable. She smiled, thinking of her job, the boxes stacked precariously all over the house. "We know she was a pack rat."

"It wasn't so bad when she was younger," Max said. "That came later. The hoarding, I mean. The house—later an apartment that she kept in town—wasn't too bad. Somehow having all this junk made her feel secure, I guess."

"I think for some people, it feels like money in the bank or something. I'm the opposite. I can't think if there's too much clutter around me."

"That's why you're the perfect person to put in charge of decluttering the place. You can put that four—"

She smacked his hand away. "I know. I can see the four. I'm considering my options."

"What options are you talking about? There isn't anything else to move."

Cold Hands, Warm Hearts 111

"Get your own deck." She moved the four. Underneath was a nine, which she couldn't use.

"If you'll hand this one over, I'll show you a variation of solitaire that's way more interesting."

Seeing as how she'd just lost, she didn't see the harm. "Okay," she said, and she collected the cards.

"My mother was the one who taught me the sixty-seven ways I know how to play cards. When I was a kid, she was always really happy and ready for fun."

Char felt a little pang in her heart. When Abby was all grown up, what would she remember about Char? *She was always really happy and ready for fun* didn't seem likely to be high on the list.

"What happened?" she asked. "I mean, it sounds like things changed."

"My father died."

"Oh."

"Yeah. They were quite a pair. It must have been like losing part of herself. Anyway, by then Philip and I were older and doing our best to drive her nuts, and suddenly life wasn't so much fun for her anymore."

"I can imagine you getting into trouble, but Philip, on the other hand—"

"Well, that's just the thing," Max said, taking the cards from her and shuffling them. "Philip has always been proper, focused, and goal-oriented, and, as my mother used to ask him, 'Where's the fun in that?'"

Char remembered Philip's conversation with her on Thanksgiving, and how he'd said his mother's side of the family had always been practical. Interesting that Max didn't have the same perspective. Or maybe his mother's *side* had been practical, just not his mother.

She was pretty sure she would have liked Mrs. Wilson a lot. As a life strategy, the pursuit of pleasure had its limits, but asking yourself *Where's the fun in that?* now and then was probably a good thing.

"But I wasn't any better," Max said, dealing the cards.

"I thought you were going to show me a variation of solitaire," Char protested, as several cards landed in front of her.

"If there are two people who want to play cards, why waste time on solitaire?"

"I agree, but I have to say that was a very sneaky and underhanded method of getting your way."

He looked up and smiled. "It's just cards, Char. Please don't read anything into my character because of it."

"Fine. What are we playing?"

"Crazy eights?" he asked. "War?"

"You're the one who's dealing. Aren't you supposed to know?"

"I'm giving you a chance to state a preference."

"That makes up for being sneaky and underhanded. What about something a little more sophisticated than crazy eights? Crazy eights I can play with Abby any day of the week."

"Ah, a woman who discerns the potential of mature companionship. How about go fish?"

She had to laugh. "Is that your delicate way of saying that none of the sixty-seven games you know are challenging?"

"Slapjack can be quite competitive," he said with mock severity.

"How about gin rummy?" she said. Who knew he had a silly sense of humor underneath it all? And since when had she found a silly sense of humor charming? "You were talking about what a grave disappointment you were to your mother."

"I was?"

"Yes. Were you extremely trying, in the usual way of adolescent males?"

"No. At least, my being a typical adolescent male didn't bother her any. When I told her I'd enrolled at the police academy, that was when she vowed to disown me."

Char looked at him over the top of her cards. "Why on earth would she do that? I'd think your mother would be proud that you wanted to be a cop. Police officer, I mean."

"Actually, I'm a federal agent these days," he said, and Char's blood went very cold. "But calling me a cop is fine. It's how I think of myself."

A federal agent? Bad enough when she had been under the impression that he was a cop in Philadelphia, on leave for reasons not stipulated. That was scary, but it wasn't an immediate threat to her. There was a limit to how much trouble a Philadelphia cop could cause her. But a federal agent . . .

"Your turn," Max said.

Char jumped, looked at her hand, looked at the pile of discards, and said, "Sorry. I lost track. What am I doing?"

Max reminded her, and she played a card.

"So your mother didn't like your becoming a cop?" she said. "Was she worried about your getting hurt?"

"That wasn't her main objection."

"Then what was?"

"She thought it was disrespectful."

"Disrespectful?"

"Pa was a gambler," Max explained. "A gentleman

gambler, as he would tell you himself. Never held a steady job a day in his life."

"You can make a living betting on ponies?"

"He was a con artist," Max said. "He'd play anything wherever he could find a mark. Pool, poker—even darts. The point wasn't to beat someone fair and square—the way I'm about to beat you," he said, playing his final card. "The point was to screw as much cash from the mark as he could, whether that meant cheating, stealing, or other larcenous behavior."

Char folded her cards. Max's father sounded something like Theodore, and yet obviously Max's mother had adored the man.

"How did your mother stand it?" she asked. "Was she really young when she met him? Or in a tough family situation?"

He shook his head as he collected the cards. "She was actually in her late twenties. She said all of her family and friends considered her an old maid and assumed that she'd missed the bus and would never get married. She worked as a bookkeeper for the water department."

"Wow," Char marveled. "She was from a good family, but this rogue came along and swept her off her feet."

"Exactly."

"And plunked her down in northern Minnesota with two kids."

"Something like that. Philip's a lot older than I am, and he remembers when they traveled around with Dad. When I came along, my parents decided to have a home base. They chose here. People don't ask a lot of questions here. They leave one another be. So long as he didn't con anyone up here, no one got into his business."

Cold Hands, Warm Hearts 115

Char could definitely see the attraction of that.

"Anyway." Max shrugged again. "The old man spent more time in jail than out of it. So what better way to prove my independence—"

"Than to become a cop," she finished. "Yes, I can see that."

"What about you?" he said.

"Me?" she said. "What do you mean?"

"I mean your family and your career. We've established that your ex is unavailable to help. What about your family?"

"I don't have one."

"No one?"

"Nope. My last living relative was an extremely elderly great-aunt who left me this cabin."

Max nodded. "You know, sometimes I've thought my family was going to drive me nuts. But it's hard to imagine not having any at all." He glanced at her and shoved the cards in her direction. "Your deal."

Max headed back across the yard to his mother's house as soon as the snow let up a little. Abby had awakened from her nap and had joined them in a hand of crazy eights, then had needed a snack, which Max took as the right time to head out. He told Char not to bother coming over until the next morning, mostly because he needed the house to himself that afternoon.

The snow, which was still falling heavily, crunched beneath his shoes. Though he had insulated work boots on, as he walked, the snow drifted over the tops and slid down past his ankles. Obviously, the purchase of actual snow boots was in his future. He would also have to find a shovel and see about making a path between Char's cabin and his house. He remembered past winters of shoveling backbreaking amounts of snow and wondered briefly how he'd ended up back here after all the effort it had taken to get out.

Once inside the house, he left his boots by the door to melt, even though tracking in snow couldn't possibly make more of a mess than already existed. Still, the mother he remembered would have chastised him for his carelessness, so he did it.

Fortunately, he'd had the foresight to pack some wool socks, so he traded his sopping wet ones for those. He took a glance at the kitchen; he knew how much work Char and Abby had been doing, yet they'd barely made a dent.

He headed upstairs. He would have spent more time working downstairs with Char and Abby instead of confining himself to the upstairs rooms, except that he was afraid he'd start enjoying himself too much, and he might forget the promise he'd made his boss. He couldn't see where that would turn out well.

In one of the upstairs bedrooms, he found the bag with the new phone he'd purchased. He knew his mother must have several phones somewhere in this mess, but the challenge was in finding them. It made more sense in terms of time expended and frustration level reached to simply buy a new one. That probably explained how this mess had gotten so bad in the first place. Instead of digging through the boxes to find whatever thingamabob she needed, his mother had probably just gone out and bought a new one.

He ripped the clamshell packaging open, only wounding himself mildly as he did so. Sucking on the cut, he plugged the phone into a jack near the baseboard, which

Cold Hands, Warm Hearts

he had unearthed the previous day, then lifted the receiver and was mildly surprised when he heard a dial tone.

From the window he could see Char's cabin. She and Abby would be doing what just now? Playing with the dog, reading a book, arguing over what to make for dinner? And he was supposed to check in with Abe, tell his boss what he had learned today and otherwise betray any trust Char might have started to have in him. He knew it hadn't been easy for her to tell him the small bit about Theodore Bainbridge that she had.

Still, he'd made a promise to his boss. On the other hand, no one said he had to check in right this minute.

He hung up the phone.

Chapter Seven

The next morning, Abby burned the toast and added too much water to the hot chocolate, but when she proudly brought it to Char, crowing, "Out of bed, you sleepyhead," Char was pretty sure she'd never eaten a better meal. Abby supervised, making sure she ate every bite, then left Char to clean up the kitchen. A reasonable trade-off, Char decided philosophically, scraping jam off the side of the cupboard.

That task finished, she pulled on her jeans, then looked out the window at the drift of new-fallen snow. She groaned at the sight and sat back down on the daybed.

"Why couldn't Aunt Kay's cabin have been in Tampa? Or Southern California?"

"Show some initiative," Abby said, pulling on her thick woolen socks. As if Char hadn't had to drag *her* out of bed ninety percent of the time.

Still, Abby was right. It was time she showed some initiative and faced up to her troubles. She collapsed back onto the bed. Or maybe tomorrow.

"Come on, Mom," Abby said, grabbing her hand and dragging her back to a sitting position. "We're going to be late."

Cold Hands, Warm Hearts

"I don't think Max is going to fire us," Char said, but she got up and finished dressing anyway.

Later in the morning, with Abby occupied, Char slipped up the stairs and into the front bedroom, where Max was actually making visible progress in his decluttering efforts.

"This is looking a lot better," she said.

"Hey, Char," he said, looking up at her and smiling, happy to see her, and her heart gave a betraying lurch. He was happy to see her! Her inner damsel was pleased and flattered. Then he said, "You want to help me move this dresser so I can get into the closet?"

"Oh, sure," she said. *See?* she told her inner damsel. *He sees you and thinks, strong biceps!*

"If we just shift it this way"—he indicated the direction with his thumb—"that'll give me enough room to get the door open."

Char nodded her understanding, took her end, and lifted. "This thing weighs a ton!" she gasped, her breath coming out in a *whoosh*.

"Just a couple of inches," Max said encouragingly, so she put her best into it. Wouldn't want him to be disappointed about her biceps. She shoved the dresser the few inches he wanted, then with a grunt dropped her end, narrowly missing her own toes.

"Okay," he said, giving her a look. "I guess that's good enough."

Char put an exploratory hand against the small of her back. Had she sprained a muscle? Herniated a disk? She straightened experimentally. No. She was going to survive.

"What is that thing made out of?" she demanded. "Blocks of iron?"

"Solid oak," Max said. "They don't make 'em like this anymore." He rapped the top with this knuckles.

"Well, give me particleboard and veneer," she said. "Geez."

"It's gotta be worth something," Max said, repeating her favorite mantra. "Solid oak?"

"But look how ugly it is," Char pointed out. "Not to impugn your mother's taste or anything."

Max waved that away, then opened the closet door and peered inside. Hastily he shut it again. Char heard the sound of falling objects hitting the wood.

"A little crowded in there?"

"Let's just say that now I know why the dresser was shoved up against the door," he said. "Wouldn't want anyone to accidentally open that door and get beaned by an old bowling ball. So." He gave a shrewd glance in her direction. "You wanted something?"

Char's stomach turned over. Maybe initiative was overrated. Maybe head-in-the-sand was a good look for her. She glanced around the room with its piles of debris still cluttering most available surfaces despite Max's best efforts, the physical manifestation of someone deeply in denial. Did she want to end up like that? She did not. The thought scared her enough that she blurted out, "I'm supposed to call the cops back."

The moment she said it and saw the look on Max's face, she wished she could recall every syllable. Stumbling a little over the words, she said, "I have a friend who mentioned that the cops back home have been trying to get in touch with me. So I checked my cell—you know how it is up here; you have to drive halfway to Grand Rapids to get a signal—"

Cold Hands, Warm Hearts

Max did something unexpected then. He just reached over and touched her hand. "Don't worry about that part. Just tell me about the cops calling."

Char took a deep breath and tried not to read more into Max's touching her hand than actually existed. For all she knew, he was trying to calm her down so she could help him shift more furniture.

"That's just it. I don't know why they're calling. Like I said, they talked to one of my friends back home and wanted to know how to find me, since I wasn't answering the cell phone and, you know, wasn't at my last known address." She gulped and tried to get her nerves under control. Which would be easier if Max wasn't looking at her that way. "Deanna didn't tell them where I was."

"Good friends are hard to find," Max said.

She had to smile at that. "You're a cop," she said. "You obviously have a different perspective on such situations." She paused and added, "I think I need your help. You know, to figure out what to do."

Max didn't respond to that directly. He said, "So what you know is . . . what? They've asked you to get in touch with them? And that they contacted your friend to learn your current whereabouts, but she didn't give you up."

She eyed him. "Exactly." Let him think what he wanted about that. She appreciated Deanna's efforts on her behalf. "Anyway." Here was the hard part. "You know I've been having some financial problems, and I've been trying to work everything out, but it's possible a creditor is impatient and trying to sue me, or something." She clenched her hands together, but Max didn't respond with judgment or a lecture about facing up to her responsibilities.

"That's not what it sounds like," was all he said, which

was reassuring on the one hand. On the other, not. "It sounds as if they have a crime that they think you might know something about it."

"Yeah, that makes me feel better," Char said, sitting down hard on the end of the bed. She raked a hand through her hair. She'd wanted Max's help. His blunt assessment of the situation was part of the deal. "I've never broken a law in my life. But my ex . . ." She shrugged. Let him read whatever he wanted into that.

There was a long silence, and then Max said, "If you want, I can find out why they're trying to track you down."

Char closed her eyes and felt some of the tension ease from her. She let out a breath. There was something reassuring about having someone in her corner, even if he was a cop.

Her eyes popped open, and she studied him. Wouldn't it be stupid if she forgot he was a cop? How did the moral of the story go? Just because you fed a scorpion didn't mean he wouldn't sting you if he had the chance. Not that Max was a scorpion, of course. Just that—

Some of her consternation must have shown on her face, because Max gave her a smile and said, "I won't give you up either."

"Why not?" Char asked, then wondered why she was pushing him. Couldn't she simply accept what he said, what he offered, and be thankful for it?

But Max's smile just deepened and he said, "Philip would never speak to me again if I did."

It was true that Philip would be upset if something Max did hurt Char, but that wasn't the only reason, or even the main reason, that he didn't want to do it. At the moment

Cold Hands, Warm Hearts

she was counting on him, which maybe wasn't the smartest thing she'd ever done but was certainly an improvement over counting on her ex-husband.

"All right," he said, trying not to notice how small and scared she looked. Char did not scare easily, and it made him feel bad. "I need to make some phone calls."

"Okay."

She didn't make any move, so he gently took her by the shoulders, turned her around, and pushed her toward the door. "I need to do this alone."

"Okay," she said again, and she gave him a little wave as she headed out the door.

The little wave was what did it. He didn't want anyone relying on him. He didn't want to be anyone's hope. That was the reason he'd decided he wasn't going back to Philadelphia after his leave was up.

But the little wave, such a silly thing, grabbed him. When there were vulnerable people—Char and Abby— and it would only cost him a little time, a little effort, to shield them, to help Char through the hardest part, what kind of man would he be if he didn't do it?

He heard her greet Abby cheerfully, and he closed the door. Then he found the phone again and plugged it back in.

He didn't get his boss on the first try, which didn't surprise him. Tomorrow, he was told, and because he wasn't eager to push it, he didn't ask for an emergency contact number.

He went back to work.

By nightfall the snowfall had largely subsided. Char called up the stairs, inviting him over for dinner. He remembered that he was supposed to stay over here tonight. He didn't want Char to think she had to keep feeding him just because he was a neighbor. But until he'd resolved the situation, he needed to keep an eye on her, as his boss had told him to. So he dusted himself off and went with them back to Char's cabin.

"Tofu?" he said, eyeing the block on the counter. It was true you didn't really know a person until you'd prepared a few meals with her.

"Yum," Abby said. "Toad food!"

Char rolled her eyes and collected a paring knife and cutting board from the drawer.

"Yum?" Max asked doubtfully. "It sounds like something we should be feeding to amphibians." He gave Abby a wink.

"It's not bad," Char said, unperturbed by his criticisms. "You just have to acquire a taste for it."

"And the reason I'd do that is?"

"Toad food is good for you," Abby said promptly.

"Lots of things are good for me, but they're not made out of bean curd."

"Do you always complain when a woman fixes you dinner? Because, if so, I can see why you're dateless and alone," Char said.

"Ouch," Max said. He shared a grin with Abby.

"She's very rude," Abby explained. She pushed a stepstool up to the counter and began pulling plates from an upper cupboard.

"Setting the table without my asking," Char said as she cubed the block of tofu. "Wow. She must really be trying to impress you."

"See?" Max said. "I do have a way with girls."

Char rolled her eyes again and tossed the tofu into the heavy skillet doing double duty as a wok. "Can you grab

Cold Hands, Warm Hearts 125

the soy sauce out of the fridge? And take the rice off the burner, please."

Abby opened another cupboard and hauled down glasses. "What would you like to drink?" she asked Max.

"We have water and water," Char added.

"Water sounds good," Max said, leaning against the counter, mostly out of the way, and doing things when Char asked him to.

She stirred the rice with a fork, then brought the saucepan to the table and measured helpings of rice onto each plate, then did the same with the stir-fry. At Max's glance, she said, "I'm not going to dirty a serving dish. This place doesn't have a dishwasher."

"That's exactly what I would do," Max said. "That's why I was smiling."

"Mom is very efficient."

"Rude but efficient," Char said. "All part of my natural charm."

Max applied himself to the stir-fry, even testing one of the cubes of tofu. "Tastes like chicken," he said. He chewed. "No, actually it's like eating a sponge."

"You heard Mom," Abby warned. "You make fun of her toad food, and you'll have to cook dinner tomorrow. She always did that with Dad—" She stopped and looked down at her plate.

"It's a deal," Max said. "I'll cook a thick, juicy, rare steak tomorrow."

"Ewww!" Abby said in horror, some of which seemed authentic. "Mom, don't let him—"

"He's teasing, honey," Char said, eyeing Max. "I think. He can make soup or beans and rice or—"

"I'll leave out the sponges," Max said, but he ate all the toad food on his plate.

The next morning at the unholy hour his boss always preferred, Max's phone rang. He barely lifted his head from his sleeping bag—he hadn't been able to completely unearth the bed yet, and once he did, he wasn't certain he'd entrust his body, precious as it was to him, to the mattress and box spring, considering a family of mice had probably lived there for several generations.

He put the receiver next to his ear and dug the sleep out of his eyes with his free hand. "What?"

The house was freezing cold. He could see his own breath when he spoke. The furnace must have gone out sometime during the night.

"Max? Where've you been?"

Max didn't respond directly to that query—no sense in having the *I quit but then decided not to maybe* conversation that would only serve to convince Abe that his time on leave needed to be extended a while longer and probably ought to include a few sessions with a shrink.

"I'm with Char Simmons," he said. "Well, not at the moment. But as we discussed." He shook the last vestiges of sleep from his brain. "She told me that her local police have been trying to reach her. I thought we'd established they wouldn't interfere."

"Theodore Bainbridge is dead," his boss said flatly.

Max sucked a breath in. No wonder his boss had wondered where he was. That was unwelcome news, although not completely unexpected, considering the kind of people Bainbridge had palled around with.

"I'm sure the local authorities just want to talk with her

about the situation. Listen, Max. We still need to establish if she knows anything about Theodore's recent business activities. There's a lot of money that's gone missing."

"Will do," Max said, though he wasn't really thinking about what he was committing to. He hung up the phone slowly. What was the best way to handle this? He sighed and dragged himself out of the sleeping bag to confront what was already turning out to be a very unpleasant day.

The morning sun streamed in through the window, and Char blinked in the brightness. It so disoriented her that for a moment she forgot where—and even when—she was, thinking it was a Kansas summer day.

Then she remembered and sat up, glancing out the window to confirm that she wasn't in Kansas anymore. The snow glittered brightly. She tried to remember if she'd ever seen sunshine up here before. Mostly the weather had been iron gray and cold.

When she opened the front door to let Cinnamon out, the frigid cold took her breath away. She'd thought the shining sun meant a warmer day—twenty-five degrees, say, or even thirty—but today had to be the coldest day yet, well below zero.

Cinnamon came darting back into the house, shivering and shaking snow from her coat, giving Char an affronted look, as if it were her fault it was so cold outside. Which in a way it was.

She rubbed Cinnamon down with a towel, reassuring the dog that she wasn't yet suffering from hypothermia. Then she checked the thermometer nailed to the tree just outside the kitchen window. Ten below. She took another look, not quite believing what she'd seen. Ten below. She'd been through plenty of Midwestern winters, but that was as cold as she'd ever been.

After breakfast, she bundled Abby up in an extra layer because of the cold, and they walked over to the Wilson house. Max had already been up and industrious; he'd shoveled a path through the new-fallen snow from their cabin to his.

An older man from the furnace repair company was already banging away in the cellar when they arrived. She knew this because, on hearing the sounds, she went to investigate. Apparently the heat had gone out during the night, and first thing in the morning Max had called for someone to fix it.

"He knows how to get results," Char said to no one in particular. She'd already called upstairs to Max to let him know they'd arrived, but he didn't answer, so it seemed he'd gone out, though she didn't know where he might have headed. The heater repairman didn't know either.

It wasn't that Max should have left her a note or anything. She didn't have those kinds of expectations, and they didn't have that kind of relationship. But still.

She shrugged and headed into the kitchen. Abby had already made a pile of trash, which she hauled out to the Dumpster.

"Brr!" she said, darting back into the house and slamming the door behind her. She came into the kitchen. Char gave her wet boots a pointed look, and Abby went back to the hall, where she made lots of noise stomping the snow off. At least that was what Char assumed she was doing.

"It's cold out there!" Abby exclaimed, rubbing her arms. Her cheeks were rosy with the cold.

"You should let me do that today," Char said. Ten below was no joke.

Cold Hands, Warm Hearts 129

"Mom! I'm fine. I was just sayin'!" She stomped over to the corner to where more trash awaited, leaving tracks of snow on the floor behind her.

Char took a deep breath and counted to ten. "I think—"

"All ready to go," the furnace repairman announced, standing near her left elbow. She jumped and whirled.

"Oh. Okay, I'll let Max know. He doesn't seem to be here right now."

"No, ma'am," the man said agreeably. "He said you'd show up before long. Sign here please."

Char scribbled in the indicated spot, said, "Hope you don't expect any payment from me," and handed him back the work order and the pen.

"No, ma'am," he said, and he tipped his ball cap at her, then ambled out the door, closing it firmly behind him. She went back to work. In a few minutes, she could feel the first beginnings of warmth emanating from the radiators.

"Much better!" she said. Abby ignored her comment, sitting cross-legged on the floor and digging through another box.

"What ya got there?" Char asked. Despite her best efforts, Abby was too chatty of a creature to be able to sustain the silent treatment for very long.

"Look," Abby said, lifting out a tattered crocheted doily. "What is it?"

"A doily," Char said. "People used to put them on furniture for decoration and to protect the fabric from getting stained and worn." She took the piece from Abby. "This one looks like it's in pretty bad shape. What do the rest of them look like? I wonder if they're collectible."

"You can find out, can't you?"

"Yep," Char said. "Why don't you just put the good

ones back in the box, and I can take the torn and really dirty ones out to the Dumpster."

"I can do it," Abby protested.

Char wasn't sure, but she knew how important it was for Abby to feel as if everything was getting back to normal, that she wasn't a victim and could do what she'd always done.

"Okay," Char agreed. "You can do it." She had to smile. What was so exciting about throwing things into a Dumpster? Still, she remembered that when she was a child, the things she liked to do would have seemed odd to an adult. Kids could be so peculiar in their fancies. As could adults, she reminded herself, thinking of her attraction to a cop—a federal agent at that.

She was taking a load to the Dumpster herself when she heard another car pulling into the driveway. She dumped the trash and closed the Dumpster lid, then stepped off the makeshift step and turned to see Max coming up the drive.

He moved slowly, head bent, as if he were watching his step. Well, it was slippery out here. They met at the front door. She looked at him, and he looked back.

The front door opened. "Why are you staring at each other?" Abby asked, standing in the hall with an armful of newspapers.

"I don't know," Char said. Then, to Max she said, "Why are we staring at each other?"

"Because I don't know how to tell you—" He stopped. "I need to talk to you privately."

Char could tell it was important, and bad, so she said to Abby, "Sweetie, I need to talk to Max alone for a few minutes. Can you stay in the kitchen? I'll come get you when we're done."

Cold Hands, Warm Hearts 131

Abby must have sensed that arguing wouldn't do any good, because she turned and went into the kitchen, a tense, small figure waiting for more bad news. Char could have cried.

She glanced over her shoulder at Max, seeking... what? But his face was closed and unreadable. She headed up the stairs, Max at her heels. Once they were in the bedroom with the door closed, Max began without any preamble or small talk.

"I went into Grand Rapids this morning and talked to the police chief," he said. "I explained you were up here, concerned about attempts by your county sheriff's department to get in touch with you. So he called down and spoke to an investigator there. It seems they'd gotten a request from Dallas to find you and question you about a crime that occurred there."

Char clenched her hands together. So far none of this made sense or seemed to have anything to do with her. "I don't know anything—Dallas? I don't think I've even been to Dallas. Ever." What had Theodore done, and how had he dragged her into it?

"Char," Max said, touching her arm. His voice was gentle, and even before he spoke, she knew what he was going to tell her. "They've found your ex-husband. He's dead."

She'd tried to steel herself to hear it, but she gasped anyway, then jammed a fist into her mouth to stop the words of shock and disbelief from escaping. She no longer loved the man, and over the years he'd done a good job of destroying whatever relationship they'd built and whatever affection for him she'd retained. But he was Abby's father.

"What happened?" she asked. Without thinking she

took his hand and tried to steady herself for the answer. The police wouldn't want to talk to her if he'd simply had a heart attack. Unless . . .

"They believe he was murdered."

Char inhaled sharply. "Oh, no. That can't be." The denial was automatic, but of course such a thing was perfectly possible. If Theodore had upset one of his more criminal clients . . .

"This will just destroy Abby," she said. She let go of Max's hand and sank down onto the nearest surface, which happened to be a packing crate. She tried to imagine what she was going to say to Abby. Growing up without a father—even one as imperfect as Theodore—would be hard. And Abby loved Theodore wholeheartedly and without question.

They would just have to do the best they could. She herself had turned out okay, hadn't she? And her circumstances had been even more difficult, because her mother had gone too.

She pressed a palm against her churning stomach. Theodore had been part of her life for so long that it was hard to think of the world without him in it.

She looked up at Max, who'd shoved his hands into his pockets and seemed to be waiting for her to collect herself.

"What—what can you tell me?"

"The police would like to talk to you," he said, not sugarcoating it or otherwise trying to make it go down easier. That was the thing with Max. He was always going to tell you exactly how things stood. Then he added, "I told them I'd ask you to come into Grand Rapids with me later today." And that was the other thing about Max. He made a plan and helped out as best he could without making a big deal of it.

Char twined her fingers together. Why did the police want to talk with her? They couldn't think . . .

"They don't think I had anything to do with it, do they?" she blurted out, her mind racing as she considered how she might prove that she'd been occupied with other problems. She knew perfectly well that an ex-spouse was always a person of interest in a situation like this. She looked up at Max anxiously, hoping he would reassure her.

"I don't know what they think," he said, and for an irritated moment she wished he *would* sugarcoat it. Then she had to smile. Why was it that the thing that you most admired about a person was so often the very thing that also drove you nuts?

He came over and next to her sat on the packing crate. Casually, he nudged her shoulder with his and said, "I'm pretty sure they would have pushed me harder if they considered you a serious suspect."

Char inhaled unsteadily at the word *suspect*. Then she reminded herself that she wasn't the one who was going to suffer the most over this. "What do I tell Abby?"

"Maybe you should wait until tomorrow," Max suggested. "After you talk to the police. You'll know more, and the hardest part for you will be over."

"Good idea," Char said, grabbing on to the idea like a life preserver. Anything to put off having that conversation with Abby. She'd never imagined having to have such a talk with Abby—not for many, many years anyway.

"So you will come in with me this afternoon?"

"Yes," Char said. "I need to get this taken care of."

"Good," Max said. "What's for lunch?"

Chapter Eight

Char could hardly eat, but she forced down some of the soup and crackers that she'd set out. Max and Abby devoured the meal. When Abby brought the dishes into the kitchen, Max said, "I asked Kate and Philip if they'd mind having Abby help out at the clinic this afternoon. That way, we can do our thing without worrying about her."

"Thanks," Char said in relief. "I wasn't sure how best to handle that. Abby will love spending some time with them." She let out a breath and forced a smile. "The sooner we get this over with, the better."

"I'm ready when you are," he said, and she was a little amused to find that she appreciated his brusqueness again. Heartfelt expressions of sympathy would reduce her to tears right now, and she needed to be calm, not distraught, to face the coming challenge.

Abby came out of the kitchen with a damp cloth and with intense concentration wiped the table down. When she was finished, Char said, "Hey, punkin', Max and I have to do something in Grand Rapids today. Max thought you might like to spend some time with Kate and Dr. Wilson at the clinic."

Cold Hands, Warm Hearts 135

"Instead of cleaning the house?" Abby asked, as if she were disappointed at the unexpected turn of events.

"It'll be fun," Char said. Then, because she could see the calculations gleaming in Abby's eyes, she warned, "Don't expect them to pay you. You can volunteer your time today."

"All right," her daughter said, heaving an exaggerated sigh.

Char smiled, and her heart skipped. She didn't want to tell Abby what had happened to her father and destroy her good-natured equilibrium. Coward that she was, she was glad to put it off for a while.

"Let's get our coats," she said.

The sky was iron gray as they walked outside, but no snow was falling. Char let Cinnamon out for a minute, then shut her safely inside the cabin and got into Max's car. Abby was already carefully strapped into the backseat.

No one said much as they drove to Grand Rapids. That was fine with Char. She was so tense, it took all of her energy just to keep from bursting into tears or shouting out her anger and frustration with Theodore.

Soon enough they reached Dr. Wilson's office. Kate swooped from the inner door to welcome Abby and invite her back to play with a cat who was being boarded and seemed bored with its owner away. Abby didn't even cast a backward glance as she followed Kate into the back room.

"Not even a hug," Char said, watching the door swing shut behind her daughter.

"Not even a wave good-bye," Max agreed. "Come on."

He opened the front door and let a blast of cold air in.

Char raced to the car and hopped in. She had her seat belt fastened before he'd even opened his door. Not that she was eager to go, just that she was freezing. Would she ever get used to it?

"Kate is a good kid," Max said, as if Char had voiced her concerns aloud. "They'll have fun. Philip will probably let her assist in examining a dog or something. She'll have a good time."

"I know," Char said. "I'm scared." She didn't know where that had come from. It was true, but she didn't need to admit it.

Max started the car and said, "I'm not surprised."

"The thing is, I feel like everything is going wrong, and if I just hadn't been such a loser—"

"Define *loser*," he said, not unsympathetically, as he put the car into drive and backed out of the parking space. "Normal human who can't control everything? Come on, Char. Everyone has tough times."

He sounded impatient, and she guessed she understood that. What was the point of blaming herself? She was doing the best she was able, and wasting energy and worries on *coulds* and *shoulds* kept her from having the strength she needed to cope with her actual challenges.

"Look," he said, glancing over at her, "if you don't encounter tough times now and then, you're not living right."

"What does that mean?" she asked. It wasn't quite the worldview she would have expected him to have, tough and competent and confident in his own skin, but of course he couldn't control everything either, or he wouldn't be here on leave.

"It means playing everything safe and risk-free isn't a

life. People who only want safety and security deserve what they get."

He spoke so forcefully that Char raised an eyebrow. "We're not even talking about me anymore, are we?"

"Does everything have to be about you?" he asked with a smile. "Yes, I'm Exhibit A."

She wondered what his story was. Obviously, he'd played it safe sometime and regretted it, but she didn't ask for details. He'd share them when he wanted. *If* he wanted.

A few minutes later, he pulled into a parking lot and cut off the ignition. Char's stomach turned over, and she wished she hadn't forced herself to eat lunch.

"This is it," he said unnecessarily.

"It looks like a library." Innocuous, possibly even welcoming.

"Ready?" Max unbuckled himself and turned to her.

"No."

"Let's go," he said anyway. He slid out of the car and pocketed the keys. Char took a deep breath and unbuckled her seat belt. Her knees felt a little weak when she stood up, but Max was at her side, and they walked up the steps to the front door together. He squeezed her hand briefly before pulling open the door.

She walked in and found herself standing in a bare-bones waiting area. The phrase *holding cell* echoed through her mind even though she knew full well that this lobby was no such thing. She stood, frozen, as Max went up to the desk officer and explained who they were there to see. It was a good thing he'd come along, because apparently she wasn't able to speak.

When Max came back to join her, she unclenched her jaw long enough to say, "I should have called a lawyer."

"Still can." He spoke in his usual nonsugarcoated way.

"Should I?" she asked, forcing the words through stiff lips.

"I'm not supposed to advise you on that."

"You're such a cop," Char said, annoyed and amused in equal measure. But at least it was easier to talk now. "What would you do?"

"I wouldn't ask the cop," Max said. Then he added, "Nothing wrong with seeing what they want and then deciding."

"Yeah, a cop would say that," she said darkly. At his look, she said, "No, you can't win. That's the nature of my neuroticism." She twisted her hands together. "You know I really appreciate your doing this. I'm just taking my nerves out on you."

"You can stop anytime and ask for a lawyer." No doubt he was used to people with nerves taking them out on him.

"Maybe this wasn't a good idea. No offense, because I'm sure you would never be involved in something like that, but sometimes bad things happen to innocent people."

"Look, they're just going to ask some questions," he said, with more patience than she'd really expected. Still, that statement sounded a lot like *This won't hurt a bit.*

"Why do those sound like famous last words?"

This time he just smiled and squeezed her hand. Probably the best course of action. There wasn't anything he could say or do that would make her feel better about this.

She chewed on a thumbnail, then decided that looking nervous wasn't a lot different from looking guilty, so she folded her hands together and started working through the multiplication tables.

"Two times two equals four," she muttered. "Two times three is six. Two times four is eight."

"What are you doing?"

"I do this to relax myself. Do I seem more relaxed?"

"Yes, Char, you seem tranquil and serene. It's going to be okay."

But it really wasn't. Theodore was dead.

She took a deep breath just as a tall, thin man stuck his head around the corner. "Ms. Simmons?"

Char straightened her shoulders. Okay, so far it wasn't too bad. "Yes. That's me. I'm here."

Max touched her shoulder. "Do you want me to—"

"Yes," she said gratefully.

"Do you mind?" Max asked the detective. Char assumed he was a detective. She didn't know. He hadn't said his name yet. "I talked to Chief Jeffers this morning," Max continued. "You're Detective Kane?"

"That's right."

They didn't shake hands, and Char wasn't sure what that meant. Maybe it meant they saw themselves as adversaries. Maybe cops didn't shake hands.

"I'll just sit quietly and observe. As long as you don't object."

"Okay," Detective Kane said. Char assumed this was cop-to-cop courtesy, because she was pretty sure if Max were her best friend or her gardener, he'd be cooling his heels in the waiting area. "But you've got to sit tight."

"Will do."

Char watched the negotiation with interest. Max treated

the small-town detective like a colleague, not playing the *I'm from the big city* card or even the *I'm a federal agent* card. Of course, maybe he'd done that yesterday when he'd talked to the chief. But somehow she doubted it. Max didn't strike her as the kind of person who had to get into scuffles to establish who was alpha dog. Of course, that might be because he thought it was perfectly obvious.

"We're down this way," Kane said, motioning for them to follow.

"Shall we?" Max said.

It was too late to cut and run, so she nodded. Max rubbed the small of her back in a discreet gesture before dropping his hand.

The detective opened the door to an interview room, which looked like an underfunded conference room—long metal table, rickety folding chairs, with a camera in one corner of the ceiling and what she suspected was a panic button on the wall.

Char pulled out one of the chairs and sat abruptly, her legs giving out a little more quickly than she liked. Max took a chair next to her.

Detective Kane stood in the doorway and asked, "Coffee?" Trying to establish a friendly environment, which Char appreciated. Unless he was trying to lull her into thinking there was nothing to worry about until he sprang out at her with "Where were you on the night of September 19?" and she wouldn't be able to think.

"Coffee would be good, thanks," she said, trying to postpone the inevitable. Her voice came out a little shaky, but the detective didn't comment, just glanced at Max, who shook his head. The detective left in search of the coffee.

"You've never had cop coffee, have you?" Max said.

She had, but there was no need to say so. "It seemed like a nice gesture. I didn't want to refuse a nice gesture."

She eyed the door, which the detective had left open. She could probably make it out to the hall before Max had a chance to stop her and talk some sense into her. She leaned forward, and Max nudged her with his arm, and she sank back into the chair.

"Three times two is six," she said.

"It would probably work better if it were harder," he suggested. "Square root of sixteen."

"Four." Then she admitted, "This is not helping, Max."

"Nothing would. But this is better than thinking all of those catastrophic thoughts you're thinking. Square root of thirty-six."

"Six. This is still too easy."

"We can do differential equations if you'd rather."

She remembered from cop shows that she was probably being observed as she sat in the room, her words recorded, for all she knew. She glanced up at the camera in the corner and lapsed into silence.

A minute later, the detective came back into the room and handed her a cup of coffee with the consistency of tar. She cradled the Styrofoam cup in her hands, saw they were shaking, and set the cup down on the table, sloshing only a little bit.

Two women followed the detective into the room. One wheeled a cart with a video camera and other equipment on it. Char gave another glance at the camera in the corner. Was it a fake one? Or broken? Or did they like to capture the suspect from multiple angles? Her palms started sweating, and she swallowed hard.

"We'll need to get this on video," the detective said.

Char didn't ask him about the camera in the corner. She noticed that Max moved his chair so that he was out of the picture. That was fine and understandable, but it meant he was farther away than she liked. She gave him a little kick under the table to reassure herself. He gave her a look that said he was making allowances for neuroticism brought on by circumstances but that he had his limits.

The woman with the equipment gave the detective a thumbs-up, and the detective nodded and said to Char, "I'm Detective Kane," although she already knew that. "Officer Ramirez," he said, pointing to the female officer who took a seat across from Char, "and the videographer, Officer Deacon. You ready Deacon?"

"Yup."

"Okay," Kane said, settling into a chair next to Officer Ramirez.

It was like facing a tribunal, though there were only two people staring at her. She was ready to confess all and fling herself on the mercy of the court, if only she had something to confess.

Kane cleared his throat, then said the day, date, and time for the record while the equipment whirred and Officer Deacon fiddled with fine-tuning everything. Then he said, "Detective Jonathan Kane and Officer Cynthia Ramirez interviewing Charlotte J. Simmons in the matter of the homicide of Theodore P. Bainbridge."

Char sucked a breath in. She'd known what had happened to Theodore, but hearing the words so formally spoken shook her deeply. Kane opened a folder and asked her to state her name and affirm that she was being recorded and that she had appeared voluntarily and had waived the right to an attorney for the preliminary questioning.

"Yes," Char agreed, and she was surprised at how strong her voice sounded. "Although I don't waive my right to stop the proceedings at any time," she added firmly. She didn't look at him, but she knew that had made Max smile.

"Now, I'm going to ask you some questions," Kane said comfortably, and Char sucked her breath in again. Max tapped her foot with his own and nodded. *Just routine.*

"I understand," Char said. Then, even though Max had signaled *just routine,* she said, "I just want to clarify that I'm not under arrest and that I'm free to leave at any time." She trusted that Max knew what he was doing, but no one ever looked after one's own self-interest better than oneself.

"You are not under arrest," Kane said, then added, "at this time," which didn't reassure her. She didn't think it was supposed to. She took another deep breath and waited. It was a good thing she'd never tried to embark on a life of crime. She would have been really bad at it.

"The Dallas police requested that the sheriff's department at your last known county of residence pick you up for questioning in the aforementioned matter," Kane said, looking at a sheet of neatly typed notes in the folder in front of him. "The Douglas County sheriff's department relayed that request to us—that is, the Grand Rapids city force—when they learned you were now living near Grand Rapids."

"Okay," Char said. She rubbed her sweating palms on her jeans. So far it sounded as if she'd been trying to evade the authorities, which wasn't good.

"The Dallas police have positively identified the body of a homicide victim there as Theodore P. Bainbridge. You are Mr. Bainbridge's ex-wife, is that correct?"

"I'm the ex-wife of a man named Theodore P. Bainbridge," Char said. "I couldn't say if the man you're alluding to is the same person."

Kane looked at his notes again. "This Mr. Bainbridge was a lawyer practicing in Kansas City, partner in the law firm Bainbridge and Cook? Missing since October?"

"That sounds like him," Char allowed.

"How long have you been divorced?"

Char supposed this was to establish the likelihood that she still harbored enough resentment to murder him. "Three years."

"Amicable? Bitter?"

Right. Like she was going to say, *Very bitter. I hated the very air he breathed.* Fortunately, that wasn't true.

"Fairly amicable," she said. "He was a lawyer, so he knew how these things could drag out. He also knew I was being very fair in my settlement request. I was the one who filed for divorce."

"The two of you had a child together?" He looked at his notes again, but apparently he didn't have Abby's name there, because he asked, "Any custody conflicts?"

"No. We agreed that I would have physical custody, and he would have ample visitation rights." So far this wasn't awful. But she knew they'd barely started.

"You cited irreconcilable differences in your divorce filing?"

That was a matter of public record, but still, it was a little creepy that they knew so much about her and she didn't know the first thing about any of them. She repressed the desire to ask Kane about his wife and children. This wasn't a social situation.

"Yes," Char said, realizing Kane was waiting for her to answer even though these were all established facts.

"What were those differences?"

How to put it? "He was a jerk and an adulterer," she said flatly. Then she caught Max's look and thought maybe she should have sugarcoated it a bit.

"And by *jerk*, you mean . . . ?" Kane asked. Char could tell that Officer Ramirez was struggling to keep a smile off her face, and that made Char feel a little better.

"I mean contemptuous of me, impatient with our daughter, concerned only with what he wanted," Char said. Her divorce attorney had told her that it was the most common complaint she heard from wives petitioning for divorce, but Char thought sharing that observation was probably unnecessary. Amazing how hard it was to answer the questions honestly without being defensive or trying to overexplain her side of the story.

"So you had a fairly amicable divorce three years ago," Kane said. He took a pen from his pocket, and made a note in the folder. What did the note say? *Nice smile? Subject appears to be lying through her teeth?* But she wasn't. She was telling the truth. She would just have to assume that would be enough.

"When was the last time you saw Mr. Bainbridge?"

"Sometime in late September. He took Abby to lunch on a Saturday."

"And at that time did he do or say anything out of the ordinary?"

Like what? Tell her he was embezzling a fortune from his law firm? "No, he seemed to be his normal self." His normal self being contemptuous and impatient, but she'd already established that. "He may have been a little more distracted than usual, but I can't say for sure if anything was bothering him or what was on his mind."

She made herself stop talking. Let Kane get on to the next question.

"Was that the last contact you had with him at all?"

Char shook her head.

"Could you please go ahead and say your response?" Kane said, but he was nice about it.

"Yes. I mean, yes, I can say my response, and my response is no, that was not the last contact I had with him. That was in early October," she said. "I called to tell him Abby wasn't feeling well. I tried to keep him informed of things like that. He was her father. So." She took another breath and said, "I also asked him to let me know when he'd pick her up for another weekend. He said he'd have to check his schedule and call me back. He never did." Her hands started to shake again, and she folded them together in her lap. "I left a few messages after that but he didn't return my calls."

"And before that? You had routine contact with him?"

"Yes. He had Abby on a fairly consistent schedule, and we always worked that out together."

"And he had been paying child support regularly?"

"Yes. The last check came at the beginning of October."

She gulped a breath down. So far the questions were easy enough. No doubt they'd get harder.

"And when the November check did not arrive, what did you do?"

There. For example, that. On the surface, it was easy enough to answer, but the unspoken question was, *Did it make you mad? Did you threaten him?* Which was ludicrous if you knew Char, but none of these people did. Except Max, and he'd known her for a grand total of about two weeks.

"In early November, when my daughter was diagnosed with a brain tumor, I tried to reach him again. I wasn't, at that time, worried about the check. When I couldn't reach him, I called his partner at the law firm. Theodore didn't have any family. At that point, I realized that there were a number of financial ramifications—he hadn't paid the health insurance premiums for our daughter, and he hadn't paid the support due at the beginning of the month. So I called the child support enforcement people, and they started an investigation."

"You didn't call the local police to report him missing?"

I'm not his keeper, she thought. *Not anymore, anyway.* Out loud she said, "I didn't know that he was missing. For all I knew, he was on vacation."

"Surely he would have mentioned that to his partner."

She willed herself to stay calm. "I never actually talked to his partner. I left a message, and he never called back."

"And that didn't make you curious?"

"I knew Theodore's partner. No, I was not surprised," Char said tartly. "Look, I didn't know what to think, but I certainly was no longer close enough to him to go to the police and say he hadn't returned a couple of phone calls so he must be missing."

Kane made a note in the folder, a lengthy one, considering how long it took him to write it. Char craned her neck, trying to see what he was writing about her, but he kept his hand curled over the paper, blocking her view.

A minute later he looked up again and said, "So you finally called the child support enforcement office."

"Yes." She made herself not respond to the *finally*. If she'd called them a day after the check was late, Kane would have suggested she was greedy. It was his job to keep her off balance, to provoke her, in hopes of shaking her if she were lying. But she wasn't, so that was going to have to be her comfort.

"Then what happened?"

"He was gone by then," she said. "Not that they've reported the results of their investigation; they just confirmed that no payment had been made, and they were unable to reach him or anyone at his law office."

"And in the meantime you haven't heard from him? Or seen him? Since that conversation in October?"

"That's correct," Char said. "A few days after I called the child support people, a friend of mine went to his house. I was up here by the time, at the hospital with Abby. My friend said the utilities seemed to be disconnected at his house. Apparently he had stopped paying the mortgage, because there was a foreclosure notice on the door. My friend said she looked in a window and couldn't see any furniture." She'd then drawn the obvious conclusion—that Theodore had intended to disappear. Maybe he hadn't gone fast enough.

"Who was this friend?"

Char glanced at Max. Deanna would probably never speak to her again if she gave her up.

"A longtime friend," Char said. "I didn't pursue matters because my daughter had become seriously ill. She had brain surgery at the Mayo Clinic earlier this month. I've been preoccupied with that."

Kane opened his mouth, probably to ask her if she could prove it, then met Max's look and didn't ask. "So you didn't file a missing persons report at that time? Or hire an investigator?"

"I don't have the money for an investigator. And no, I didn't file a missing persons report. I was worried about my daughter and our financial situation. Theodore's absence seemed planned. There was no sign that he'd been hurt or kidnapped or anything dramatic."

Kane nodded, not that he agreed with her, just signaling that he'd heard her. He leafed through his notes, then said, "So this contact you had with Mr. Bainbridge in October. What date, exactly, was it?"

Char blew out another breath, then closed her eyes and thought back. "Abby usually went with him the first weekend of the month, so I called to confirm. That was when he told me he'd have to check his schedule. It would have been the first Wednesday of the month."

"Ramirez, do you have a calendar?"

Ramirez already had a datebook open and was paging through it. "That would have been the third of October," she said, turning the book around and showing it to Char.

"That sounds right," Char agreed.

"Was the conversation in the morning or the afternoon?"

"It was evening," Char said, glad that her conversations with Theodore were intermittent enough that she could remember a thing like that. "Around seven. I called him at home. It's a long-distance call from where I was living, so I can look it up on the phone bill for the exact time." *I can prove it,* she meant. Max smiled, and she kicked his ankle. What did he know? Had he ever felt this defensive in his life? Ever had a reason to?

Kane didn't say anything. Not that she'd really expected

him to take her up on her offer. She supposed if they needed the information, they could run it down without her help. Subpoenaing records from the phone company for a homicide case ought to be fairly easy and wouldn't require her cooperation at all.

"Now," Kane said, and Char could tell from his alteration in tone that he was finally getting to the crux of the matter and that all the questions about missing persons reports were just a way to get warmed up. She straightened and paid even closer attention to what he was saying. "In your conversations with Mr. Bainbridge, did he ever talk about being in debt or needing a lot of money?" He paused, then continued. "Fearing for his safety if he didn't pay a creditor back?"

"No," Char said promptly. "He lived as if he was affluent, although he was careful not to gloat about his income to me. I think he was afraid I'd go to court for more child support if he really lived it up while Abby and I were barely getting by. But no, he never talked about money with me."

She'd known he had every right to be frightened by some of his clients, and she wouldn't be surprised if he'd gotten into financial trouble in one dodge or another, but he would never have said so to her.

"You say you know his law-firm partner?"

Char blinked. That wasn't the follow-up question she was expecting, but—

"Not well," she said. *Leave it at that.* She hadn't liked him personally, but he hadn't been a bad man. No need to drag him into this. Whatever had happened to Theodore hadn't been his partner's fault.

Cold Hands, Warm Hearts 151

Kane didn't respond. He looked at the folder in front of him again.

"Where were you, exactly, in early November? Say, from the first through the fifth. When you say you were up here, what do you mean by that?"

"I was in Rochester with Abby. In the hospital."

"Okay," Kane said, and she didn't offer to produce medical records and eyewitnesses to confirm her continual presence at Abby's bedside. Let him ask. But that wasn't what he asked next. "Do you have any of Mr. Bainbridge's records or belongings in your possession?"

"No." Her answer was quick and her tone vehement. She gave an awkward smile. She'd been extremely careful not to have anything at all of Theodore's, and she wanted to make sure no one ever suspected that she might know something she didn't.

"Okay," Kane said again. He looked at the folder some more. "I think that's about it for now."

Char started. That was all? She tensed. Sometimes just when you thought you could relax, that was when the catastrophe happened. Not that she was paranoid or anything. She waited, because no one had made a move to leave.

"Where are you staying?" Kane's pen was poised over the paper in the folder. Char hesitated. If she told him and it became part of the record somewhere, then other people could find her, such as the people who'd made Theodore run and who'd apparently killed him.

"You can reach me through your colleague, Max Wilson," she finally said. "But I have a question for you. How do you know this . . . body is really Theodore? I mean, who identified the body?" She knew it was a strange question, but she had a reason for asking.

Kane didn't answer right away, obviously calculating the risks of telling her anything. Then he shrugged and said, "Apparently they matched dental records."

Her stomach turned. Now she felt sick for a different reason. "What happened that he could only be identified through dental records?" She couldn't believe she hadn't asked about the details before, but when Max had told her Theodore had been murdered, she'd just assumed he'd been shot by one of the thugs he represented.

"Burned in an apparent warehouse arson." He paused. "After he was shot in the head." So there could be no doubt he'd been murdered and it wasn't an accident.

Even so. "I just can't imagine that happening to Theodore," Char said.

"You mean you can't imagine anyone wanting to murder him?" Kane looked skeptical, which meant he knew more about Theodore than he was letting on.

"No, I can imagine that. I just can't imagine he'd let anyone close enough to shoot him." Her stomach turned again as another thought occurred to her. "Where's his partner?"

Kane shifted in his chair but didn't say anything.

"He's missing too, isn't he?" Char guessed. "Look, a couple of years ago we took Abby to one of those police-sponsored child-safety things. You know, where you do that swab and keep it in case the cops ever need your DNA? Well, Abby was pretty little and didn't know what to do, so Theodore showed her how to do the cotton swab, fingerprinting, the whole thing. I still have Abby's packet. I think I have his."

Kane raised an eyebrow.

"Dental records can be faked or switched," Char said. "But I have his DNA."

Kane glanced at Ramirez, then back at Char. "Bring it in," he said. "We'll see what we can do."

Max lingered for a moment to talk with Kane, while Char made a beeline for the door once she realized she was free to go.

"Does she really think . . . ?" Kane asked.

Max shrugged. "I'm not sure exactly what's on her mind. I'll bring that sample in if she can find it. You'll let me know if you need to talk to her again?"

"Sure. Don't think Dallas will have any questions I missed, but you never know what might come up."

Max nodded and went after Char, who was already pushing open the front door and heading to the car.

"Wait a minute," he said, catching up with her on the front step outside the station house. "What brought that up? I have to admit, you surprised all of us when you suggested that Theodore might not be dead."

"I know Theodore," Char said, as Max unlocked the door and opened it for her. "And I think he was planning for this day for a long time."

"What do you mean?"

"He's a planner, Theodore is. If he embezzled all of this money from the law firm and liquidated all of his assets, you can be sure he would have fled the country. He would have plotted it very carefully. And he wouldn't have been caught."

She got into the passenger side, and Max went around to the driver's side.

"I suppose it's possible, Char. But isn't it a lot more likely that he got crosswise with one of the unsavory types he represented? That he'd gotten some threats and so he started planning to make an escape, take a break, but was too late?"

"Not Theodore."

Something in her tone made him stop what he was doing and turn to look at her. Her ex-husband had really done a number on her, hadn't he? She was seeing conspiracies where there weren't any. What kind of relationship had they had? He'd seen this kind of denial before in his work, and it usually stemmed from deep-seated fear of the deceased. He tried to keep his voice as gentle as possible when he spoke again.

"Char, he's dead. I know it was a shock, that it's still a shock, but he's not—he's not an enemy anymore. There's nothing he can do to you. He can't get you."

"He was never my enemy," Char said. "He was just not the person I thought he was. That's why I left him."

Max heard in her voice that she meant it. Considering all the trouble the man had caused her over the years, that was far more a tribute to Char's character than anything else.

"I'd like to punch him for leaving Abby when she needed him most, and for sticking me with the medical bills, but that doesn't mean he's my enemy. I'm sure he never realized the harm it would cause. He never knew Abby had a brain tumor." She wrapped her arms around her waist. "I didn't like his clients or the trouble they caused him—us—but that was weakness on his part, not malice toward me."

Max knew weakness could be more dangerous than malice—because you so often underestimated what a weak

Cold Hands, Warm Hearts 155

person was capable of doing—but he didn't say so. What purpose would it serve to frighten her? He was silent for a moment, thinking about all she'd said.

"Okay," he finally said. "So explain to me why you think he's not dead."

Char studied him for a long moment. He supposed she was wondering if he was asking as a friend or as a cop. He wished it were as black-and-white as that. He wished if she asked which it was, he would have a ready answer.

"Theodore specialized in assets protection," she said, which probably meant she'd decided he was a friend. He was glad, but he was also concerned that there might come a time when his being her friend would come into conflict with his being a cop. He hoped, when that time came, if that time came, he would make the right choice. Whatever the right choice might be.

"Tell me about that," he said, and he started the car, thinking it might be easier for her to talk if he wasn't concentrating his full attention on her.

She looked out the window, and he wasn't sure she was going to explain, but then it appeared she was just organizing her thoughts because she said, readily enough, "At the most extreme, unethical end, assets protection includes taking money that rightfully belongs to a creditor—or someone else—and disappearing. Even faking a death to get people off your back."

Max nodded, keeping his eyes on the road and not saying anything. It wasn't his area of expertise, and he knew it wasn't successfully accomplished very often, but it was always possible, he supposed.

"He advertised estate planning. Wills and trusts, you

know? Assets protection doesn't have a great reputation, so it's not like he advertised the service. But that's what he did."

And that was what had gotten him into trouble. While there were certainly legitimate businesspeople who had legitimate reasons for sheltering assets, it was the kind of thing that would attract the attention of people who, at the less harmful end of the scale, didn't want to pay taxes and fraudulently developed strategies for avoiding them, as well as the attention of people who, at the more harmful end of the scale, were involved in the illegal drug trade and wanted to launder cash.

"What about his partner?" He was missing too, which made Char's claims a little more credible. Two missing men and one body meant one man hadn't been located yet. And if authorities were looking for the wrong man . . .

Char shrugged. "I never liked his partner much, but he struck me as a lot more ethical than Theodore. I know they had many disagreements over the kinds of clients Theodore was bringing into the firm."

"So you know for a fact that Theodore engaged in unethical practices?"

"Max. He committed adultery more times than I can count. If you can't keep a promise you made to your wife, how ethical can you be?"

"Good point."

"Besides, I know for a fact that he showed other people how to hide their assets and fake their deaths."

Chapter Nine

Char felt a headache coming on as she and Max went into his brother's clinic. She could tell that Max had a plethora of questions about what she'd just said. She'd been trying to explain why she thought the way she did, but she hadn't intended to suggest she knew more about what Theodore had done in his legal practice than she did.

And at the moment she didn't want to think about or talk about any of it.

Max closed the door quietly behind them. The chimes had rung but without resulting in the appearance of either Kate or Dr. Wilson, so Char leaned over and pressed the buzzer on the front desk. After a moment Kate came through the inner door.

"Hey, guys," she said politely, obviously having been warned to keep her usual joie de vivre under control, considering the difficulty of what Char and Max had been doing. "Abby's assisting my dad at the moment," she added. "They're giving Ranger a bath."

That sounded like the kind of messy good fun Abby would enjoy. "And Ranger is . . . ?"

"Dad's Labrador," Kate said. "How's Cinnamon doing?"

"She's fine," Char said. "Almost back to normal. By the way, I've got a check for you." She'd set aside some money from the amount she'd earned for helping Max with the cabin. She reached into her bag and withdrew her checkbook.

Kate glanced at Max, lifted an interrogatory eyebrow, took in Max's shrug, then said to Char, "You don't owe anything. Your bill has been paid in full."

Char dropped the checkbook back into her bag. "Let me talk to your father, Kate. I appreciate the intention but—"

"It's not Dad," Kate said. "If you need a further explanation, talk to him." She jerked a thumb at Max and hurried through the inner door before Char could stop her.

"I think she expects me to yell at you," Char said, watching the door swing shut behind Kate. The kid could move fast when she was motivated.

"Are you going to?" Max asked, as if he was genuinely curious although not particularly worried. "I don't like being yelled at on Tuesdays."

The absurdity of the statement interrupted what she'd wanted to say. She hadn't had any intention of yelling, per se, but now she couldn't even remember the point she wished to make.

"Well," she said. "*Should* I yell at you? I'm just trying to discern your motivation."

"Would you believe me if I said I had embarked on a personal-development program that involved performing random acts of kindness on Mondays?"

She couldn't help the smile that tugged her lips. "No. You strike me as the kind of man who considers himself already developed enough. Give it another shot."

"I found several hundred dollars on the sidewalk and couldn't think of anything else to do with it."

Char propped one hip against the counter and gave him a look. She still wasn't used to the idea of Max having a silly sense of humor. Unfortunately, it only made him more attractive.

"No," she said. "You would have turned it in to the police."

"I am the police," he reminded her. "So I did."

She didn't feel like arguing with him about the bill anyway, or protesting what he'd done, or setting him straight about taking paternalistic actions in regard to her without first asking permission. Which meant that his strategy had worked, no doubt exactly as he had intended it to.

"Well, whatever your motivation, thanks. I do appreciate it, although I hope you bargained a discount out of your brother."

"I just told Philip that you were working a lot harder than we were paying you for."

"Hmm," Char said. "That's true enough."

"Actually, I suspect it's Abby who's doing the hard work."

She smacked him on the shoulder—not that there wasn't some truth to what he was saying—and then the inner door swung open, and Kate and Abby came through, Abby chattering a mile a minute. She looked a little damp, as if she might not have gotten out of the way of a Labrador shaking excess bathwater off its coat. Spotting Char, she turned a megawatt grin on her and said, "Guess what happened today?"

Char tried not to think what would happen to that grin when Abby found out about her father. Still, there was no need to tell her just yet. Not until Char knew for sure what had happened.

"I can't even guess. What happened?"

"Dr. Wilson was called out to look at a horse that fell down an old well."

"Fell down a *well*?" It sounded just improbable enough to be true. Char glanced at Kate to make sure Abby—or Char—hadn't misunderstood, and Kate nodded her confirmation.

"My goodness. That poor horse. Then what happened?" She didn't think it could be anything too tragic, or Abby wouldn't be so excited about telling the story. Although you couldn't always tell with kids.

"They got the horse out—that was before they called us—but we had to go see if the horse was okay."

"And was it?"

"No," Abby said. "It broke its leg."

That didn't sound good. Char asked apprehensively, gently, in case Abby was about to share something sad with her, "What happened then?"

"The owner asked Dr. Wilson to put it down." Abby looked over at Kate. "I didn't know what that meant, so I asked Kate. Do you know that it means to make an animal dead?"

Char cleared her throat. Why did these conversations always have to show up out of the blue? "Yes, honey," she said. "Sometimes when an animal is very sick or very badly hurt, the vet has to do that so it doesn't suffer."

"That's what Kate said."

Char glanced at Kate. Surely they hadn't let Abby be part of that kind of procedure, not without talking it over with Char first? Of course, things were different up here.

She wasn't the only one who was living close to the bone, and here a working animal that couldn't work could be an unbearable financial hardship.

"But Dr. Wilson said he couldn't do that because of his policy."

Char blew out a little breath of relief.

"Then Kate had to go back home and hook up the horse trailer, and we loaded the horse—Nightstar—into it," Abby chattered on, "and Dr. Wilson brought him to his farm, and I got to see all of his animals again." Abby's eyes were shining as she relayed the story. "And the goats let me pet them. He said we could come by anytime."

"Yeah?" Char said. "That's nice of Dr. Wilson."

"Then I helped file some folders and clean up around here," Abby said. "And then I helped Dr. Wilson give Ranger a bath because he got stinky while we were loading the horse. Then Kate said you were here. And now I'm wet and hungry."

"Wet is your own fault, but hungry I can help you with," Char said, finding Abby's coat and hat bundled onto a chair in a corner. Her mittens had disappeared, which required instituting a search. They turned up on the floor beneath the reception counter, Abby disclaiming all knowledge of how they could have gotten there. Once she'd gotten Abby zipped up, Char said, "Say thanks to Kate and Dr. Wilson."

Abby did so, pushing open the inner door and shouting out to Dr. Wilson, who called back, "Don't forget to review the difference between *canine, feline,* and *equine.*"

"Dog, cat, and horse!" Abby crowed, and she let the door shut.

They went out into the gray day together. Abby agreed that a McDonald's meal would solve her hunger problem but only if she could have a chocolate milkshake to bolster her strength after such a busy afternoon. They munched the meal in companionable silence as Max, who had declined the temptation of a Big Mac, drove them back to the cabin. The light was waning as they pulled into the drive.

"I bet Cinnamon will be glad to see us," Abby said, racing ahead of Char but thwarted in her attempt to be the first inside by the locked front door.

"We'll be over in a bit to do some work," Char said, getting out of the car. Max nodded, then backed the Buick and turned, heading toward the Wilson house.

Char unlocked the front door to the cabin and couldn't help giving a little wave to Max, which she really, really hoped he didn't see. Cinnamon darted out the front door to do her business, yapping at Char for making her hold it for so long.

A few minutes later, Char and Abby walked over to the Wilson house to get a few hours of work done before bed.

"I'm upstairs," Max called out as Char shut the front door behind them. She looked around the place. It was warmer and, with the lights on, certainly brighter and somewhat less messy than it had been. But despite its simple elegance, it still didn't seem welcoming. Not exactly a place she'd want to live. She wondered what had really made Max interested in staying there.

She set Abby to work in the kitchen, then climbed the steps to talk to Max. She knew he wouldn't let his questions about Theodore remain unanswered for long, so she might as well get it over with.

When she walked into the bedroom, Max was unpacking a box filled with torn and motheaten blankets.

"Those aren't worth anything," Char remarked, finding a few square inches on the bed to sit down.

"I know. I'm just surprised anyone would save them, so I wanted to find out if they'd been used to cushion something else." He peered into the empty box and shrugged. "But no such luck." He shoved the blankets back into the box, then nudged another box with his toe. "This is a bunch of old books. Are they worth anything?"

"Depends," Char said. "I'll take them downstairs. I'm stacking books in a corner of the kitchen, now that there's some space there." She bent down to heft the box and bring it downstairs.

While she was in the kitchen, she directed Abby to the next chore—sorting through a box filled with comic books and old mail.

"Comic books may be worth something," she explained. "Old junk mail is not." She demonstrated the difference while Abby, predictably, rolled her eyes. Then Char kissed the top of her head and went back upstairs.

Max had opened another box and was peering into the interior with a perplexed expression on his face. When she came into the room, he rocked back on his heels. Now he said, with no more small talk or assignment of petty tasks, "While Abby's busy downstairs, tell me what you meant about your ex."

Char sighed. She supposed they had to do this right now.

"I'll take the DNA sample into Grand Rapids tomorrow," Max bargained. "I can convince them that it's important to take it seriously."

"Why does this matter to you?"

"You're kidding, right?"

"It's just that—I should have understood Theodore's character a lot sooner than I did," she said. "It makes me seem stupid. Or culpable."

"You're not responsible for other people's actions."

It wasn't as simple as that, and they both knew it, but she appreciated his saying it. She moved restlessly to the window and looked out into the twilight. The lake had frozen over now, and there was no pleasant sound of lapping waves, just the sound of the wind sighing through the trees.

"Okay," she said. "Theodore. When we were dating, he had what I thought was the endearing quality of trying to impress me with his brains." She tried to think of how to explain. "It was like, he thought I was really smart, and he wanted to show that he could hold his own with me. It was flattering."

At Max's disbelieving look, she said defensively, "I was young. I didn't know the difference."

"Well," Max said. "I guess some of us have to learn things the hard way."

"Ouch," Char said, but the remark made her feel obscurely better. "Anyway, he would come over in the evenings after work and tell his war stories, and I would be suitably impressed." It was hard to believe how young and ridiculous she'd been. At least she didn't have to worry about that anymore. Although, as it turned out, age hadn't seemed to make her any wiser. Look at her, baring her soul to a federal agent.

"And during one of those occasions . . ." Max prompted, before she could change her mind about telling him all this.

"Right. During one of those occasions, he gloated about how he'd helped a client disappear, despite some considerable debt and an outstanding warrant or two. He claimed he couldn't be compelled to testify because of attorney-client privilege."

"I'm not sure that's true in cases of fraud," Max said. "But someone would have to know about it first to push to prosecute it."

Char shifted from one foot to the other. "I was young enough to think that he was just sailing a little too close to the wind. Because he could, you know? Like it was an experiment, the way you drive too fast when you're a teenager." She realized she was sounding defensive and went on without the explanations. "I know he did it more than once, because he told me. I told him what I thought. I didn't judge him, I said, but I thought he needed to reflect on the kind of person he wanted to be."

"And so he stopped confiding in you about things like that," Max guessed.

Char could practically see Max filing away the information for later use. She expected he would tell it to the cops tomorrow. Well, let him. Better him than her.

"Exactly. I thought he'd come to his senses and realized that while the things he was doing were technically legal on his part—I don't know for sure, but he always claimed they were—they weren't right. I thought he'd stopped."

"But he hadn't."

Char shook her head. "No. Although I didn't realize the extent of what he was doing until after Abby was born. Then it was hard to know the right thing to do. I had to think about it for a long time before I realized that I was condoning his behavior, endorsing it, you know? And I couldn't let Abby grow up with two parents who'd lost their moral compasses." That came out more pompously than she'd meant, so she gave Max an apologetic smile.

"Do you remember any names?" was all he said. "Of clients he did this for?"

"No," said Char. "He never named them. He just called them 'the rich factory owner' or 'the priest who got into trouble.'"

"The priest?" Max echoed.

"Yes, I remember that one pretty clearly. That was one of the first. It was very successful. He had the man go on a mission to Mexico. I guess there are districts there where, for the right price, the officials will produce a death certificate and a newspaper story about the death, although no actual body."

Max grunted, so Char assumed he knew what she was talking about.

"That's it?" he asked.

"You mean, do I have evidence? Of course not. That's why I didn't bring it up in the questioning this morning. I don't have anything to back up what I'm saying. I didn't want to sound like a vindictive ex-wife, you know?"

"Okay," Max said calmly, and Char realized she'd raised her voice without meaning to. She took a deep breath and forced herself to relax. "I was just curious," he continued. "You seemed pretty sure that Theodore couldn't be dead. Then when you sprang this on me—it just surprised me."

"I know, it seems way out there, doesn't it? Faking a death? But Theodore's self-preservation instinct is extremely well developed. I always figured he was willing to settle with me during our divorce proceedings not because he was such a good guy but because he didn't want me to go through with a formal discovery process."

"There are plenty of men who should settle but don't. Egos get in the way."

"Having a healthy self-preservation instinct means setting aside your ego sometimes."

"Except when you're being indiscreet and telling your girlfriend about showing clients how to fake their deaths."

"Sure, but that's different. That's trusting the person you're romancing and trying to impress her. That's infatuation, you know? Infatuation can make even intelligent people do stupid things."

"That's true," he said with enough vehemence that he had to have fallen victim to infatuation and its attendant stupidities a time or two himself. "But if he was planning to use the techniques himself, he would have been wiser to keep quiet about it."

"Sure." Why was Max trying to establish that Theodore had done stupid things? Then she understood with a jolt that he was doing what Theodore had done, only in a much different way. He was trying to establish that he was smart, smarter than Theodore. It had nothing to do with the case. It had to do with her. She was a little flattered, which meant she hadn't learned much from her experience with Theodore.

Maybe Max didn't even realize he was doing it, but he was; he was acting like an infatuated fool, although his foolishness wasn't quite as foolish as other people's might be. She relaxed a little, leaning a shoulder against the wall, and said, just to play devil's advocate, "But this was eight or nine years ago. He wasn't planning to disappear then. He wasn't planning anything for himself then, except to pull in the big bucks until retirement."

Max stiffened. Oh, now, she really shouldn't have added that last. Men could be goofy about money and earning power. Didn't he realize that in a competition between Theodore and him, he would win without even having to try?

"Hey," she said. "You know, I may have been young and dumb once, but that is a curable condition."

He looked up and met her eyes, and she knew from the smile he gave her that he understood exactly what she was talking about.

Max had misled Char about his intentions. Well, hadn't misled her, had lied. He had no intention of following up on the interest that sparked between them. And he had no intention of bringing DNA evidence relating to Theodore Bainbridge's homicide to the police in Grand Rapids.

Instead, on the following morning, he brought the kit to the Minneapolis field office and talked to the special agent in charge there, having already called his own boss to explain what had happened. Abe had whistled through his teeth and made whatever calls needed to be made and pulled whatever strings needed to be pulled to get the evidence Char had provided them analyzed and compared to the remains the Dallas police were dealing with.

"You sticking close to her?" Abe had asked, and Max admitted he was. He must have also admitted, without meaning to, that sticking close to Char wasn't exactly a hardship, and his boss had chuckled and said, "It would be a real mistake to underestimate a woman like that."

Which meant what? Max wondered and brooded all the way home.

And it wasn't until he unlocked the front door to the house that he realized how many years it had been since he had considered anyplace home.

Chapter Ten

"What furniture do you plan to keep?" Char asked. It was Saturday morning, and they had finally gotten most of the front bedroom cleared. She pressed a hand to the small of her back and rubbed.

Max was silent for a moment. "I hadn't really thought about it," he said finally.

Char shrugged and opened a trunk, letting the question go. "Look!" she exclaimed, pleased and surprised as she lifted a piece of clothing out. "I think this is what they call a pinafore." The dress was clean and only slightly wrinkled. White cotton ruffles accented the neckline and hem. "Abby would look so cute in this."

"Abby would never wear that," Max said, which was true. Abby tended toward jeans and sweatshirts—tomboy clothes. Although did anyone call rough-and-tumble girls tomboys anymore? The world had changed a lot from when Char was a kid. Thank goodness.

Char set the dress aside, then knelt next to the trunk to go through it more carefully. The clothes stored away in it were all clean and neat. Some were worn but carefully mended. The smell of camphor was strong and grew stronger as she reached the bottom of the trunk.

"Were these your mom's?" she asked.

"I don't know," Max said, giving the clothes a cursory glance. Well, what did she expect?

"Okay to sell them?"

"Who'd buy them?"

"Vintage clothes are popular. Kids' clothes are hard to find—people really wore their clothes out a couple of generations ago."

"Fine by me," Max said, getting up to stretch. "Knock yourself out." He gave a glance around the room and said, "It's hard to believe how hard we've been working when it still looks like this." He hesitated and said, "She must have stored everything here when she moved into her apartment. I thought she'd gotten rid of most of her junk. But she just brought it here." Another pause. "I wish I'd known."

From his tone, Char could tell he wished a lot of things. "You haven't been here in a while, then?"

"No."

Impulsively she touched his shoulder. "Didn't have much contact with your family?" she asked. Just because she wished she had one didn't mean families didn't have their problems.

"No. We haven't talked much in the last ten years," Max said.

Char rocked back on her heels. *Ten years.* "Until . . ." she prompted.

"Until I went on leave." The way he said it was like closing a door.

"And you went on leave because . . . ?" Char ignored the closed door.

But he must have meant his closed door, because he just shook his head and turned away.

Monday Char and Abby drove all the way to Rochester for a follow-up appointment with Abby's neurologist.

Abby clutched her stuffed Dakota, although she had, in general, outgrown comfort toys. Still, Char was tense, and no doubt Abby had picked up on that.

The appointment was quick and much more cursory than Char had expected. They hadn't been in Dr. Ash's office more than ten minutes when he said, "Everything looks great. We just need a follow-up appointment next year."

"Next *year*?" Char squawked.

"Sure. Unless, of course, you see any troubling symptoms. We've talked about those: seizures, headaches, that kind of thing." He smiled and stuck out his hand to shake, and it was wonderful news and also scary. She'd relied on Dr. Ash to guide her through all of this, and now she was really on her own.

Here was another beginning, as frightening and as full of promise as all beginnings were.

Char felt a little at loose ends when they got back home. "Hey, Abby, let's go for a walk," she said. That'd help her to settle down. They could check the mail and get some exercise.

Abby agreed, and they bundled up against the cold.

The mailboxes were about a mile away down the winding Silver Lake Road, which was barely wider than a car, bordered by birches and pines so tall, you could barely see the tops.

"What is that?" Abby finally asked. "It sounds like someone opening a door."

"That's the trees. They creak when the wind blows them."

"They're not going to fall on us, are they?"

"Of course not," Char said, with more confidence than she felt. Abby put her hand in Char's as they walked. Char could feel the trust in the gesture and hoped she was worthy of it.

A rustling in the trees made her glance to her left. She saw the flash of white that meant a deer was running from them. She hoped she wouldn't run into a male elk or other creature that might decide to scare her off his territory.

She gripped Abby's hand more tightly. A gentle snow started falling as they walked. It looked like glitter on Abby's knit cap.

"It's snowing, Mom," Abby announced, as if Char might not have noticed. "Can we go sledding?"

"If it snows enough," Char said, but the snow stopped before they reached the mailboxes. They picked up the mail and returned home.

"I wish it would snow more," Abby said.

"It will," Char said.

Char had mentioned a doctor's appointment in Rochester, and Max had had to fight the urge to ask if she wanted him to accompany them. That was going beyond sticking close and was a lot more personal than he should get.

The phone rang, and he caught it on the second peal. It was his boss, who said shortly, "No match. The body in Dallas is not Theodore Bainbridge."

The words landed like a punch. Max had known Char

Cold Hands, Warm Hearts 173

was convinced that Theodore was still alive, and now she was proved right. So it was a question of, had she told Max everything she knew? Or was there another reason she believed Theodore was alive? And was it because they were in contact with each other?

But if so, why would she have told Max she thought Theodore was alive? They couldn't be in any kind of conspiracy together, or she would have kept her mouth shut. Still, it was curious.

"We need a meeting," Abe said.

"I don't like leaving here just now."

"This has been kicked up the ladder, Max. It's not up to me."

Char and Abby came home a few minutes later, and he hoped Char would come over and tell him how the appointment had gone, but she didn't. A few minutes later, he saw the two of them head up the road for a walk, and he had the impulse to catch up with them and go on the walk too. But under the circumstances, he should probably keep his distance.

The next morning, a sharp knock on the door surprised Char while she was pulling her socks on. Cinnamon barked, wagging her tail frantically to alert Char to this anomaly.

She peered out the front window. Max. His car was in the drive, still running, so he'd just dropped by. For what?

One way to find out. She opened the door. From the way he stood on the stoop, she knew something had changed.

"It's Theodore, isn't it?"

"May I come in?" he asked. "I'll only be a minute."

She nodded and stepped back, then shut the door behind

him. Awkwardly she brushed a stray curl behind her ear and said, "I can make some coffee."

"I have to go. I have a flight to catch."

"Oh."

Abby came into the main room just then, in jeans and a sweatshirt, but she hadn't brushed her hair yet. She gave Max an accusing look and said, "Where are you going?"

"My boss wants me at a meeting in Washington, DC," he said, speaking as much to Char as to Abby.

Char put her hand on the back of the chair nearest her. "Is it because . . . ?"

"Yes. I'll call when I know more."

Of course she didn't have phone service, but she understood what was happening. He was sliding back into his professional mode, and she was someone suspect because of her relationship to Theodore.

It wasn't the first time she'd regretted the relationship she'd had with Theodore, and it probably wouldn't be the last, but she'd thought a little better of Max.

"You'll be back, right?" Abby asked Max anxiously, and Char's heart went out to her. It would be a long time before she stopped believing everyone might disappear the way her father had.

"I should be back by Friday," Max said.

In the window behind him, Char saw that snow had begun to fall.

"All right. Well," she said. How did you let someone know you understood he was cutting you loose when you'd never had any indication that he got attached in the first place?

"Friday, Char," he said, and he reached out and took her hand.

Cold Hands, Warm Hearts

Char cleared her throat. *Don't let him get confused,* Dr. Wilson had said, which would be easier if she didn't feel confused herself.

"Well," she said again.

"I'm not going to be reassigned to full-time active duty yet, Char."

"Okay," she said.

"I'll be back," he said, and Abby giggled and said, "You sound like that movie." And then the awkwardness and tension was gone, and she was just standing next to a friend who had some work to do. Her daughter would need breakfast in a minute. There wasn't anything confusing in any of that.

But then Max touched her cheek and kissed her gently on the lips. Then he was gone, closing the door gently behind him.

"Well, darn," Char said softly, watching his retreating back.

"Oh, ick," Abby said.

"I think we need a sled run," Char said after Max had gone and they'd eaten breakfast and she'd convinced Abby to brush her hair.

"Yes!" Abby exclaimed. "Bundle up," she told Char. "Last time you got cold too fast."

Char smiled at her daughter, who someday was going to be appalled that she sounded just like her mother. They sledded for an hour, until Abby complained of being cold and relieved Char of having to call a halt to the festivities herself because her toes were frozen solid.

"Hot chocolate?" she asked. "Race you to the cabin."

They reached the front door at the same time, Char hampered by her conscience and the unwieldy sled she was carrying, which she propped against a wall of the cabin. Then they went inside for hot chocolate.

A tall, slender man was seated in the easy chair in the living room. Char and Abby both stopped in their tracks. Char dropped a hand to Abby's shoulder. This couldn't be good. No. This was very, very bad.

"Char, Abby," the man said with a charming smile. "I'm so glad to see you. Are you glad to see me?"

"Dad?" Abby said incredulously.

"May I have a hug?" Theodore said to his daughter. After all of Abby's complaints about not seeing her father in so long, Char was a little surprised that she wasn't more excited. But then, Abby had been through a lot without her father there, and she was old enough for that to matter. Abby gave him a cool look and didn't run immediately to his side.

Instead, she pulled her coat off, hanging it up carefully, then pulled her boots off and left them on the mat by the door, being neat and methodical in a way she never was when it was just her and Char. Finally, she took her hat and gloves off and put them in the wicker basket on the shelf. Char followed her example, moving as mechanically as Abby. When she'd stowed the last glove away, she turned to deal with her ex-husband, squaring her shoulders and reminding herself that if she could manage everything she had already managed, she could manage this.

Abby went over to the daybed, where Cinnamon was licking her favorite toy—some guard dog she'd turned out to be—and pulled the Pomeranian into her arms. Now

Cinnamon barked, when it was too late to warn anyone about anything.

"I called you," Abby said to her father.

He turned to look at her, his movements a little jerky, like a puppet on a string, and Char saw the tension that vibrated within him, the desperation that he was trying to hide under his usual facade of *I have everything under control.*

"I know, sweetie," he said, as if he were reading the lines, an actor not very gifted in his sphere.

"I need to talk to your daddy," Char said to Abby. "Can you go into the bedroom and read for a little while? I'll come get you in a minute."

Abby looked from her face to Theodore's and back, and then she scooted off the daybed, picked up Cinnamon, and went into the bedroom, shutting the door behind her.

Char's mind raced. What was he doing here? And how could she get him to go away without causing any more damage than he'd already done?

"So what brings you here?" she asked him. "Apparently rumors of your demise were greatly exaggerated."

"Indeed. Well, it seemed the only option open to me at the time," Theodore said, a charming smile still on his lips. But Char wasn't fooled.

"What brings you here?" she repeated. He couldn't possibly think all he needed to get out of trouble was a smile. Could he?

"Deanna told me where you were." That didn't answer the question. It also wasn't true.

"Deanna doesn't know where I am," Char said, and then she could have bitten her tongue off. Challenging Theodore on his lies was a dangerous business, and she should know better by now. What she had to do was get him out of here—or, alternatively, get herself and Abby out of here. She wished she and Abby had skipped the sledding and gone right to the Wilson house to work. If Theodore had confronted her there, at least she could have phoned for help.

"You didn't tell Deanna?" Theodore raised an eyebrow. "Then it must have been Janice."

Of course Janice didn't know either, but Char kept her mouth shut. They both knew he was lying. The question was, why? Clearly he had tracked her down somehow and had gone to a great effort to do it, and it wasn't because he wanted to spend time with his daughter.

"So what happened to Abby?" He gestured toward his own head as if to indicate the scar Abby had there. Char had been wondering if he'd even noticed. He was just self-absorbed enough to have missed it.

"Well, if you've talked to Deanna and Janice, you know what happened," Char said, then set her jaw. She needed to be smarter about dealing with him. They both knew he was a liar and a manipulator; she didn't need to score points off him to prove it. It wasted energy, energy she needed to find a way to get out of this mess.

"Humor me," Theodore said, and there was something new and unwelcome in his tone. Char was glad that Abby had retreated to the bedroom.

"She had a brain tumor," Char said, not mincing words. "You stopped paying the health insurance premium. I sold everything I owned to pay the bills. I owe everyone thousands of dollars. End of story."

"So you're up here because you're out of money?" Theodore asked.

She noticed he didn't say he was sorry or ask the prognosis for Abby. He was here about money. Which was unfortunate for him, because she didn't have any.

"Yes," she said.

He leaned back in the chair and watched her out of eyes she didn't recognize anymore—flat and expressionless.

She was starting to feel afraid.

"I suppose the Dallas death didn't convince you," he said, steepling his fingers together, as if they were discussing a less-than-convincing turn onstage at the community theater. "I thought it was well done."

He would. "You like your precious neck too much," Char said. "I knew when you disappeared that sooner or later I'd hear about your unfortunate and untimely death, and I knew I would have to actually see your body to believe it. Who was it in the fire? Your partner?" Then she realized what must have happened, and she took an involuntary step away from him, toward the room where Abby—the most precious, vulnerable thing in her life— likely sat reading a book about a princess.

"Was it?" she whispered.

"Yes."

"Did you—" No, she wasn't going to ask that. She swallowed hard. "He was shot through the head and burned, Theodore." She could hardly get the words out. Her hands shook, and she reached for a chair and sat down hard before her legs gave way. She had thought Theodore was capable of a great many things, but not that. She'd assumed, if anything, it had been one of his unsavory clients who had done it and he'd simply taken advantage of the situation.

"He was the one who stole all of the money," Theodore said, as if that made murder all right. "He made it look like *I* was the one who did it."

Char stared at him, not sure what to believe. Theodore had been methodically liquidating his assets, starting several years ago. She realized that now. He'd been setting cash aside for some reason. She hadn't been surprised to learn that the law office's bank accounts had been emptied. Naturally, she'd assumed he'd done it. He had probably intended to. Maybe his partner had caught wind of what he was planning and had beaten him to it?

"I had to run—some of that money belonged to my clients, people who weren't going to be very understanding if I tried to tell them what my partner had done. I didn't have enough money. I tried to get him to tell me where it was, and he wouldn't."

Char felt her heart hammering in her chest. He'd just admitted killing someone, and now she and Abby were alone in a remote cabin with him, with no way to call for help.

"So what are you doing here?" he asked cheerfully, as if he hadn't just admitted to murder.

"Here? In the cabin? Trying to survive."

"Why?"

"Why what? I told you, you let the health insurance lapse, so I owe thousands of dollars—tens of thousands of dollars—"

"Money?" Theodore laughed. "Are you really—you mean, you don't know yet?" His smile broadened. "That's terrific. That's just great. You don't know."

"Know what?"

"The whole purpose of this charade was for you to file the life insurance claim."

"What are you talking about?" Char demanded.

"Don't you remember? We agreed that I'd maintain a life insurance policy until Abby was grown, so that if anything happened to me, she would still be able to go to college."

Char tried to breathe. "You didn't pay the health insurance premiums. It never occurred to me that you'd lived up to any other obligation."

"Well," he said, and he shrugged. "I need you to file that claim."

"I would, Theodore," she said. "Except you're alive, and it would be fraud."

As she spoke, she thought she heard the sound of a vehicle on the road. Who was it? Did Theodore have a partner? Or had someone followed him here? If anything happened to Abby . . .

"I don't have any money."

"Not my problem," Char said.

"Ah, but it is."

"What do you want?"

"I'm going to take Abby," Theodore said. "And you're going to file the claim and share the wealth with me."

"No."

"Yes." He reached into his coat and withdrew a pistol.

Char caught her breath and stepped back. "Theodore, don't do it."

"I don't think you're in any position to dictate to me," he said.

A flicker of movement out the window caught her eye.

Max. She forced herself not to look, not to hope. If it was Max, she had to give him a chance to help her. If it wasn't, then her situation had probably just gotten a lot worse.

Should she tell Theodore that the police knew he was alive? Would that make him run off—an outcome she certainly wouldn't regret—or would it provoke him into some other rash action?

She heard the whisper of sound as the outside cellar door eased open. She'd never put the padlock back after loading wood through it. She was glad of the oversight now.

"How much is the policy for?" she asked. "I mean, if I'm going to commit fraud and risk my own freedom, it had better be for more than fifty grand or something ridiculous like that."

Char had never been a money-motivated person, and it was out of character for her to act as if she was now, but she was betting Theodore wouldn't notice.

And he didn't. "It's one-point-five million, Char. You'll get your share."

His eyes flicked away from her face, and she knew Max had come up behind her. Theodore raised his pistol, and Char shouted, "He's got a gun, Max!" and she threw herself to the floor. Theodore rose from the chair, took a stumbling step forward, and then Max was wrestling the gun from him, and it was over.

Detective Kane listened to her story, taking careful notes. Officer Ramirez had already hustled Theodore into the backseat of a patrol car. Abby was at Char's side. Char had one arm around her daughter. Cinnamon was in Abby's lap, barking to alert them to the presence of the cops.

Cold Hands, Warm Hearts 183

Max came to sit next to Abby, protecting her, protecting them.

"You want to make some hot chocolate in the kitchen with me?" he asked Abby. "While your mom does this?"

Abby glanced at Char.

"Go ahead," Char said. "You and I will talk later." She glanced up at Max. "She was really brave. I know she was scared, but she did just what I said. I'm very proud of her."

Abby nodded. "He didn't seem like Daddy. I knew Mom was worried."

"I'm proud of you too," Max said. "So how about that hot chocolate?"

"So why are you back so quickly?" Char asked. "You barely had time to get to the airport."

The cops had gone, Theodore with them.

"I resigned."

"What?"

"I resigned. I don't want to be a cop anymore."

"Okay," Char said.

"Okay?" he echoed.

"Well, elucidate if you must," she said with a smile. "You saved the day, and now you're telling me you quit being a cop, when it's obvious you were born to do it."

He got to his feet and paced to the window, looking out. How many times had she seen him do that? The watcher. How could he think he was done being a cop?

"I was almost all the way to the airport when I realized I had a choice," he said, rubbing the back of his neck. "I could stick with you until the situation was resolved, even if you were somehow involved in Theodore's dirty dealings, or I could do what my boss had asked me to do."

She was quiet for a moment. Then she said, "Well, I'm glad you picked me. But why does it have to be an either-or thing?"

He shook his head. "I can't hesitate when I'm supposed to be doing my job, Char. That's what this leave was about in the first place. And here I am, still hesitating to do my job."

She wasn't so sure that was what it was, or that it was a bad thing, but all she said was, "Tell me."

This time he did, still staring out the window, not looking at her. "I was investigating a case with my partner," he said. "And here's the dealer, and here's me, and here's my partner." He drew squares on the frosty windowpane. "I'm in the lead. Dealer makes like he might be reaching for a gun."

"Okay," Char said.

"But I don't *know* that he's going for his gun. So I hesitate."

"And he *was* going for his gun."

"Yes. And he shoots us both."

"Max. I'm sorry," Char said. She was on her feet now, reaching for his hand.

"My partner had to retire on permanent disability."

"I'm sorry," she said again. "It sounds awful. Did you ever nail the dealer?"

"Yes, but that's not the point."

"I'm sure I don't have to tell you that you weren't the one who pulled the trigger."

"That's what the shrink said. But that's not the point either."

"Okay. Tell me what the point is."

"The point is, I hesitated."

Cold Hands, Warm Hearts

"Uh-huh," said Char.

"And it cost my partner. Big-time."

"And you're giving up the job because you hesitated? It doesn't occur to you that maybe that's a good reason to *keep* the job? It's the cop who shoots first who kills innocent civilians."

"Shrink said that too."

"Then what do you want from me?" Char asked.

"How about, 'Hey, glad you're not moving back to Philly this week. Let's figure out what you're going to do with the rest of your life'?"

"Okay," Char said, sliding a little closer to him. That she could do. "First of all, you're going to unresign. Then you're going to take full credit for nailing Theodore, not let these cowboys act as if they had anything to do with it. Then we're going to finish cleaning out your mother's house and sell it. This place too."

"Yeah?"

"Yeah. I'm very practical. This place did what it was supposed to do, but, honestly, I'm not going to live on a remote lake in a falling-down cabin for the rest of my life."

"You should try Philly sometime."

Char smiled. "Yeah, I think I just might."

Cinnamon barked as Abby returned with the hot chocolate, and Max leaned over and kissed Char.

"Oh, ick," Abby said.